Books by Allan W. Eckert

THE GREAT AUK

A TIME OF TERROR

THE SILENT SKY

The Silent Sky

PASSENGER PIGEON

From *The Birds of America* by John James Audubon, Copyright, 1937,
by The Macmillan Company. Reproduced by kind permission of The
Macmillan Company.

The Silent Sky

*The Incredible Extinction of
the Passenger Pigeon*

A Novel by

ALLAN W. ECKERT

AN AUTHORS GUILD BACKINPRINT.COM EDITION

AN AUTHORS GUILD BACKINPRINT.COM EDITION

Published by iUniverse.com, Inc.

For information address:
iUniverse.com, Inc.
620 North 48th Street, Suite 201
Lincoln, NE 68504-3467
www.iuniverse.com

Originally published by Little, Brown & Company

ISBN: 0-595-08963-1

Printed in the United States of America

There are many wild creatures living now which future generations may never see except in pictures or museums. The green sea turtle, the California condor, the grizzly bear, the Everglades kite, the whooping crane and even the symbol of America, the bald eagle, are among the numerous species whose very existence hangs in precarious balance today. To those men and women who have devoted themselves to the preservation of these and other forms of wildlife this book is humbly and sincerely dedicated.

ALLAN W. ECKERT

Dayton, Ohio
January, 1965

The Silent Sky

PROLOGUE

I*T was just about noontime on an autumn day in 1813 when the great artist and naturalist John James Audubon set out for Louisville, Kentucky. This was a journey of fifty-five miles from his home in the town of Henderson on the south shore of the Ohio River only a short distance from Evansville, Indiana.*

Hardly had he begun traveling when there came a great sound from the north and he turned to see a tremendous flock of passenger pigeons coming his way. They stretched out of sight to east and to west and he could see no end to the flock in the north.

The birds flew very close together and in such a thick blanket that "the light of noonday was obscured as by an eclipse," and he had considerable difficulty keeping his frightened horse under control. The air was heavily impregnated with the odor of the birds.

Audubon followed the river road to Louisville, arriving there at sunset, and all this time the birds had continued flying past in undiminished numbers. The river banks were crowded with men and boys who were shooting incessantly at the pigeons, which flew quite low as they crossed the wide expanse of water.

Curious as to how many birds might be in this titanic flock, the largest he had ever seen, Audubon carefully calculated the number in a segment only one mile wide and three miles long traveling at a rate of sixty miles per hour (which was the normal cruising speed of passenger pigeons), allowing two birds to the square yard. He arrived at the conclusion that from the time he had left Henderson until he arrived at Louisville, a total of no less than one billion, one hundred fifteen million, one hundred thirty-six thousand birds had crossed the Ohio River, and that such a flock would require eight million, seven hundred twelve thousand bushels of food per day . . . and this was only a small part of the flock which took three full days to pass. The total number of passenger pigeons in this southward migrating flock would undoubtedly have been a virtually incomprehensible figure.

That a creature with such a tremendous population could have been made extinct at all is difficult to believe, and yet, almost exactly one hundred years after this day, the passenger pigeon had ceased to exist.

I

THE morning was balmy and the air, after a night's heavy rainfall, was redolent of moist earth and new growth. Fine crystalline droplets trapped by long gray streamers of Spanish moss in the oaks reflected early sunlight in tiny sparkles. Nearby, a bobwhite whistled crisply and a distant crow cawed hoarsely for company. A beautiful day was in prospect.

Yet the peace of this southern Alabama countryside in mid-March was not apparent in the actions of the cluster of forty passenger pigeons on the ground at the fringe of a deep woods. In all but one of these birds there was an obvious undercurrent of nervousness and, while they continued their rather desultory feeding begun at daybreak, mostly they milled about aimlessly.

The single exception was the largest bird of the company, a handsome male who crouched quietly facing the south, his attitude one of patient listening. He had been in this position for nearly an hour, but now there came an abrupt change. Although he remained crouched, he raised his head high, craned his neck and cocked a brilliant scarlet eye skyward.

His attitude was noted and almost immediately emulated by the others. From far in the distance came a whisper of the sound that had stirred him — a low murmur, as of a breeze rustling through a willow — and then low to the south appeared a flight of birds like a single puff of dark smoke.

A wave of excitement blossomed in the grounded birds and a number of them began nodding their heads in a curious rotary fashion while others shuffled about in little circles, their trembling wingtips barely brushing the ground. The group's attention became divided between the approaching flight and the large male bird, and there could be no doubt that he was the leader.

Within minutes the swiftly flying birds had reached them. They were several hundred feet high and in a dense oval formation containing no less than a thousand individual birds. The big male threw back his head and a strange screeching cry left his ebony black bill, a cry reminiscent of two tree branches creaking together in the wind, wholly unlike that of dove or domestic pigeon.

The cry was echoed by many of the passenger pigeons above them, exciting the forty even more. Several of them flapped their wings, as if anxious to join the flight now rapidly leaving them behind, but the leader merely resumed his posture of patient waiting. This was not his first migration and he knew that flock was only scouting for the main body, which would be coming along before much time passed.

On eight different occasions in as many years this fine bird had made the long flight from Deep South to far north, and he was too experienced to waste his energy now in aimless wing-flapping or circling. He closed the bright eyes encircled by a ring of lavender featherless flesh and allowed his head to hunch into a restful position on his smoothly feathered shoulders. In this pose he seemed somewhat smaller, if no less regal in bearing, and his detachment transferred itself to some of his companions who snuggled down and dozed near him.

It was just a little after six in the morning, and the striking metallic iridescence on the large male's nape and shoulders changed colors magically as the angle of the sunlight increased; from golden bronze to burnished green and then to a lovely opalescent bronzed purple. He seemed to revel in the warmth of this new sunlight which bathed his gray back. Here and there that gray showed a faint tinge of olive brown, and his back was lightly speckled with a scattering of tiny brown-tipped feathers like little half-moons. His long, sharply tapered tail touched and — except for a fringe of startling white — blended with the brownish gray of the earth.

Not until nearly an hour after the flight of scouts had passed, however, was his most eye-catching aspect apparent as he suddenly stood up alertly on ridiculously short red legs. From the light powder-blue of his throat to the reddish-fawn of his belly, his breast was a rich red in color, only slightly deeper than the red of a robin's breast. Now he stretched to his full eighteen-inch length and cocked his slate-blue head toward the south, and his streamlined body became rigid and similar in contour to an elongated frozen teardrop.

The sound which had caused this reaction came clearly to all of them; it was a sound of thunder — an unceasing, powerful but muted thunder, a great vibration of the air which caused the very soil beneath them to tremble.

The passenger pigeons were coming.

Out of the south they came and the flock was immense,

stretching for miles to east and to west. They were at least twenty birds in depth and behind the leading edge the flock was endless, dissolving from compacted individual birds in the van to a heavy deep gray cloud behind. It was as if somewhere to the rear a vast forest fire raged and its dense smoke was being borne by a stiff south wind.

As they came nearer, the sound grew to frightening proportions, an incredible bombardment to the ears, as if a thousand churning sternwheelers and a thousand clattering threshing machines and a thousand trains rumbling through covered bridges were all approaching at once.

As the front of this expansive cloud passed five hundred feet over them, the big leader catapulted into the air. His strong pointed wings, spanning a full two feet, cupped the air and thrust it behind effortlessly, and he was instantly followed by the others.

In moments they had intercepted the multitude several hundred yards behind the leading edge, easily matching the sixty-mile-per-hour speed established by the leaders. So closely together did they fly that each bird's head was only inches behind the tail of the bird preceding him, his wing tips all but touched those of the birds to right and left and no more than two feet separated him from the birds above or below. Yet despite such a tight formation there was no confusion, there were no collisions. There was in fact a remarkable unity of movement as each bird predicated his own actions by those of the birds in front of him as well as those at his sides and both above and below.

The sound of the individual passenger pigeon's wingbeats was slight, but when it was multiplied by the incredible number flying here the air was filled with an overpowering roar. Perhaps for this reason they mostly refrained from vocal sound.

The dung from these birds fell constantly and hit ground and trees in a steady hail, marking their passage as clearly as if a speckledy whitish line had been drawn beneath them as they flew. In addition it filled the air with a characteristically sharp odor which often remained for many hours after they had passed.

The handsome leader became dissatisfied with his position after they had flown only a few miles, and he dropped from the main column. In the open space beneath the bottom layer of birds he put on a burst of speed and swiftly overtook the leaders, his wings angling sharply to the rear and pumping closer to his body the faster he flew. There was no objection from the birds here at his approach and no confusion as they unhesitatingly jockeyed position until there was room for him in the line. Even among these leaders he was an impressive bird, though by no means the largest.

Flying in the forefront was not quite as easy as in the main body of the great flock, where already the blanket of air had been broken and was being pulled along with the thrashing of wings. This suction became so pronounced that farther back in the column a distinct wind was created which even caused the taller trees below to rustle their young leaves.

Nevertheless, his strong measured wingbeats hurtled him

along smoothly and effortlessly. Now and again fatigue might cause one of the leaders to drop down and rejoin farther back, with his place taken by one of those flying immediately behind him, but this was not a matter of concern to the vigorous male. He was in excellent condition and it would take many hours of constant flying to affect him in such manner.

His own little flock was by no means the only flock to join this mass migration. Frequently, as they arrowed northward, other flocks intercepted them, some as small or smaller than his own but others numbering in the hundreds, even thousands. Once, an hour or so after moving into his lead position, he watched as another flock fully five hundred yards wide and easily six times that in length angled in to their right like a peculiar fluttering ribbon and merged with them.

So thick was the flock and so heavy a shadow did it cast that on the scattered farms over which they flew the chickens actually began heading to roost, and horses in the fields pulling plows and those on the roads pulling wagons or buggies bolted in panic.

During this initial flight the shape of the great flock was gradually changing. It narrowed and stretched considerably farther behind, forming a very heavy column two miles wide and forty birds or more in depth. The rear remained out of sight. Every now and then the column would split around high hills, but mostly they stayed close together in a vast thundering line.

To any observer on the ground it must surely have seemed that every passenger pigeon in creation flew in this single flock. Yet this was only one of a half dozen or more migration flights of similar size. From central Texas on the west to northern Florida's Atlantic coast on the east, the passenger pigeons were heading north. The great migration had begun for all of them.

They had been flying for almost four hours when a group of perhaps twelve dozen birds shot toward them directly from the north but made no attempt to merge. Instead they flared as one bird three hundred feet ahead, reversed direction and paced the larger flock. Then they began angling downward and the flock followed.

The handsome leader scanned the vast unbroken expanse of forest stretching out before them. Even as he watched, a gray-blue cloud of a thousand or more passenger pigeons burst out of the trees and sped off to the north. He checked his own speed along with the other leaders, and they sailed across this newly abandoned area at a height of one hundred feet above the trees and a speed of no more than thirty miles per hour.

It was obvious where the smaller flock had been feeding. In a roughly circular area the early-leafing trees were much less fully leaved and the branches and ground were coated with the deep blue and white droppings of the birds. This was where the advance contingent had stopped to feed and rest, and a sudden hunger manifested itself within the big leader.

As soon as the already fed-upon area was passed they dipped sharply and leveled off mere feet over the tallest trees, although continuing their flight. This lowering and slowing of the front of the column had a curious effect. As a thin trickle of water sliding down a slight incline spreads into a pool at the bottom, so now the birds behind began overtaking their leaders and spreading out in a massive cloud that grew to seventy, one hundred, five hundred birds in depth at the front. When forward progress slowed even more the build-up of birds increased until the cloud overhung a circular area with a diameter of twenty miles . . . and still it trailed out of sight behind!

At last the lead birds began settling into the uppermost branches of the trees and swiftly dropped downward limb to limb until they were upon the ground. These trees were mostly newly leaved hardwoods — beech and oak, primarily, but with a scattering of hickory, walnut, sassafras, butternut, dogwood and others — and the beating wings knocked much of this foliage off.

The disturbance created by the birds as they alighted was awe-inspiring to behold, and the animals of the forest scattered in terror. The overwhelming noise from the thrashing wings became accompanied by a weird eager cry, a piercing "*keek keeeek keeeek.*" Every branch, every foothold on every tree was filled in a moment with pigeons and then overfilled as still more came. Finding no perching places open they simply alighted upon the backs of their companions until the birds were stacked four and five and sometimes even a dozen deep.

As if the din of their wings and shrieking cries was not enough, more racket developed as dead branches with masses of birds as thick as hogsheads on them snapped and crashed down with terrific noise under the weight. Occasional explosive thuddings were not uncommon as whole dead trees up to two feet in diameter toppled with a load they could not bear and hundreds of birds clinging like swarming bees to the branches and each other were crushed when they struck.

Not only the birds on these trees were hurt, for each time a branch broke under excessive weight it smashed to the forest floor and crushed dozens of birds already there. Surprisingly, the survivors paid scant heed to the numerous birds which lay dead or dying around them.

More fortunate were the pigeons which landed in limber saplings, for these would bend rather than break, their tips gently arching until they touched the earth, only to spring upright with a loud swish when the birds leaped off.

One of the first to land on a tall hickory a foot in diameter, the large leader was quickly boxed in by hundreds of birds on all sides. This tree grew from the very edge of a severely undercut creek bank and as the weight became more than it could bear it began to lean and the bank crumbled. There was a faint popping of bracer roots and the tree went over as if in slow motion. It hit the ground with scarcely more than a light jarring and immediately the male hopped lightly to the forest floor.

The ground surface was a conglomeration of decaying leaves, twigs and moss. In and atop this litter was liberally strewn the basic sustenance of the passenger pigeon — beechnuts. These tiny triangular nuts that had matured last fall also hung in large numbers still in their burs on the trees and were dislodged in a steady pattering by the continued fluttering of the pigeons through the branches.

The big bird's head bobbed with the regular cadence of a

metronome, and at each nod a beechnut was found and swallowed. Frequently he came across acorns under the leaves and these he swallowed greedily. Still clinging low to the ground on tangled vines were wild grapes, hard as pebbles and scarcely more than wrinkled skin over seeds, and he ate a dozen of these.

Here he uncovered and devoured an earthworm and there a pair of beetle grubs. Every once in awhile he would nip off a fresh new sprig of plant growth pushing up through the debris. Although his tiny red legs were useless for scratching through the surface covering, his probing black beak missed little.

. In a quarter hour he could eat no more. His crop was swelled to such an extent that it looked as if he had attempted swallowing an apple and it had lodged in his throat. This did not hamper his movements, and when he found a momentary opening he flew up to the branch of a tall beech where he sat close to the trunk twenty feet off the ground. As soon as he was able to do so he flitted to the next higher branch, avoiding the most congested areas.

The continuing racket made by the feeding birds and those still arriving was deafening. Bits of foliage torn from the trees and dry leaves from the forest floor whirled through the air along with a blizzard of downy feathers, all held aloft by the turbulent wing-spawned whirlwind.

Close to the top of the beech tree the large leader stopped and crouched on a firm branch, resting his beak snugly on the huge rounded cushion of his crop. Despite the noise and confusion raging about him, he gave voice to a queer contented chuckling and then closed his eyes and dozed.

By the end of another half-hour the deep shadow cast by the birds began to lighten as further arrivals decreased. There now appeared to be as many perching pigeons as feeders, and every branch of every bush and shrub and tree was lined shoulder to shoulder with them, mostly sleeping but many filling the air with that complacent chuckling.

The ground below remained hidden by a moving blanket of birds picking up every last morsel of anything edible and the latecomers had begun appeasing their hunger by plucking off the fresh buds of various trees. It was about this time that the large leader's eyes opened and he fluffed his feathers.

His swollen crop had diminished in size by about a fifth and abruptly he defecated a viscous blue and white material, adding his little to the inches-thick coating already on the ground and lower branches. Then he sprang from his perch and climbed above the treetops.

Already several hundred birds were circling, and he joined them feeling vigorous and refreshed. To the south the hordes of pigeons continued to arrive but these birds settled in the woods miles to their rear. The main column itself continued to stretch endlessly into the southern horizon.

Within five minutes the circling birds numbered in the tens of thousands and without further ado they struck out to the north. Even above the beat of the wings close to him, the large leader heard the great thunder of rising birds in the woods below as those that had already eaten and rested sufficiently followed.

At this point the migration took on the pattern it would maintain for the remainder of the journey — a width of approximately a mile but only two or three birds deep. The birds gave no thought to the many hundreds of dead and injured they were leaving behind, not through callousness but simply because this was nature's way.

Skimming along at a mile per minute several hundred feet above the Cumberland Plateau of the lower Appalachians, they crossed the sprawling Tennessee River at Hobbs Island in north central Alabama and then followed the river basin upstream, crossing into Tennessee just twenty-five miles west of Chattanooga.

Where the Clinch River emptied into the Tennessee they began following the smaller river, which went upstream in a more northerly direction, then branched again to follow the Powell River where it joined the Clinch. Up this river valley they flew through the Cumberland Gap and into Kentucky.

They continued without pause over the rugged brier-clad Kentucky hills, and the big leader's wings beat methodically, mechanically, tirelessly. He could, if need be, maintain this pace for twenty hours or more without resting further. But on this flight it wouldn't be necessary, for they were nearing the single overnight stopping place of the migration. Upon meeting the upper Licking River near West Liberty, they followed the stream northwestward and began to settle as they reached an appropriate area near Falmouth early in the evening.

The mountains were now far behind the front of the flock and the tree-blanketed rolling hills of the past hundred miles or more provided far more roosting space and food than this great flock or a dozen others like it might be able to use, although food was not to be a major concern of this stop. All winter long these birds had fed well in the South, and a layer of fat had built up under their skin. If necessary it could have carried them all the way from the Gulf Coast to Canada without too seriously weakening them.

The large leader was not particularly tired and so he was not first to begin the downward angling to roost, but he followed the movement instinctively when it began. It was very cold out and many of the slopes were covered with the residue of a recent snow, which glowed a pinkish blue reflection of the sunset. The trees stretched naked arms toward them in greeting and the birds dipped down to receive that embrace.

This time there was no pile-up of birds as there had been at the mid-morning feeding place. The entire line of birds stretching out behind settled wherever it happened to be, and one of nature's odd phenomena developed — a continuous mile-wide band of pigeons roosting tightly side by side in trees and shrubs all the way back to the Alabama border.

Feeding for the lead birds and those still in the mountain country was a difficult proposition, for the snow covering on many areas hid the fallen nuts and seeds and the buds were still tiny and hard and bitter, not yet swelled with the gentle caress of spring.

The large leader chanced to be in an area relatively wind-swept of snow and there were enough leftover autumn acorns

[17]

and hazelnuts to partially fill his empty crop. He also ate a quarter-ounce of grit composed of sand and small pebbles for the benefit of his gizzard in the crushing and pulverizing of these hard shells. In those areas covered with snow, however, the birds made no attempt to feed and merely settled for the night on their perches, falling asleep at once.

The morning's flight began just at dawn, and in the first rays of the newly risen sun this incredible ribbon of birds crossed low over the Ohio River at the eastern outskirts of the largest city on their route — Cincinnati.

Pigeon migrations were not unknown to most of the residents of this famous river metropolis, but usually they were seen at a distance and flying over unpopulated countryside. Seldom had the birds passed over the city's perimeter in such fashion and at such low altitude and the populace took advantage of it.

With surprising speed the word spread and the rooftops and streets became alive with men and boys firing into the column at random. The birds were easily low enough for successful shotgunning and these weapons — loaded with extra-heavy charges of small lead shot, nails, bits of metal and other material — brought down scores of birds at every discharge. Some of the people used rifles and others even wielded bows and slings or threw rocks by hand, but it was the shotguns which accounted for the greatest toll.

The shooters gave out long in advance of the supply of birds. They had killed many thousands of them but it was as nothing to the flock. When, early that afternoon, the leading edge of this mile-wide column approached a likely looking nesting area near Big Rapids in west central Michigan, the tail end of the flock was just then completing its passage over the Ohio River, three hundred twenty air-miles to the south.

In this single flock of passenger pigeons there were no less than *two billion* birds.

2

THE passenger pigeon was hatching.

Exactly thirteen days ago, almost to the hour, this single pure white egg an inch and a half long had been laid on the rickety platform of loosely woven twigs. The large leader and his mate had shared patiently in the job of incubation, and not once during those days had the smooth and faintly glossy egg been exposed to the air for more than a few seconds at a time.

Now, however, as it moved sharply with the exertions of the baby bird within it, the female immediately fluttered off the nest and alighted a few inches away on the branch which held it. She tilted her head to one side and stared expectantly at the little egg with a red-orange eye.

She was a delicate bird, this female, even more streamlined than the large male who had wooed and won her several weeks after the flock's arrival here, but considerably smaller than he and not as brightly colored. From the tip of her dull gray beak to the end of her tail she was just under sixteen inches and of a dusky brownish-gray rather than the clear blue-gray of her mate. The touch of iridescence on the back of her neck and shoulders was much less evident than the male's, and her breast was more of a grayish-rust.

Within the egg the baby passenger pigeon flexed his little body again and strained against the thin walls which imprisoned him. Abruptly the shell clove in half, and a wave of cool, damp air engulfed him. He scrambled frantically, pushing the shell halves farther apart, and then sank back exhausted on the intertwined twigs.

There was unfortunately little to admire in his appearance. With the exception of his bill, which was greatly oversized and practically the length of his body, he was only half as long as a man's thumb. And when this ungainly black-tipped bill opened, as it did now, it was very wide and it seemed incredible that the tiny bird could keep from turning himself inside out.

There was none of the parents' elegance in this little fellow. His ugly, lead-colored skin was only sparsely covered with damp, hairlike, yellow feathers which clung to his sides. His feet and legs were weak, unable to support his weight, and the miniature naked wings were ridiculously frail. His great bulging eyes were encased by thin bluish lids, each with a pin-head-sized hole in the center over the pupil.

A faint whisper of sound came from his throat, and the female jumped to the edge of the nest. With two rapid flicks of her bill she flipped the egg halves to the ground forty feet below and then she straddled him and crouched.

At once a pleasing warmth shut away the mid-April chill from his tender skin and he snuggled comfortably against her, his bill projecting from the downy feathers at the base of her throat.

A moment later this bill tip was nudged and he strained forward instinctively. His beak entered hers, followed by his entire head, until it appeared she was swallowing him. A warm, heavy fluid suddenly erupted in her throat, and he opened his mouth eagerly and swallowed a large quantity of nourishing milk similar in texture and color to thick cream. The only real difference between this and mammalian milk, in fact, was that the pigeon milk contained no sugar.

In this first feeding it actually took little of the nutritious fluid to fill the hatchling, and he withdrew his head, snuggled back under the blanket of warmth she created and slept. Every few hours this feeding process was repeated, and life for the baby passenger pigeon during those first six days was little more than a matter of eating and sleeping and growing. Once in awhile he was dimly aware that the female had left the nest, but her place was taken right away by a somewhat larger bird who was just as warm and soft and whose milk was just as thick and plentiful and good.

That this pigeon milk from both male and female was highly nutritious was evident in the rapidity of his growth, for during those six days he more than quadrupled his size, and the only thing relatively unchanged about him was his beak. Since it had remained virtually the same size as it was at hatching, it no longer seemed so grossly oversized.

Little feathers now covered his body, and though the yellow filament feathers still stuck through them all over and imparted a decidedly ludicrous appearance, the gray of his skin was no longer visible. On the tips of his wings, on his stub of a tail and on the short upper legs a few pinfeathers were showing. He was still undeniably ugly but in his size and unflinching gaze, at least, there was the promise of adult beauty. As his feathers formed a sleek coating, his body lines lost their lumpiness, except for his belly, which remained constantly distended with milk.

His eyes were wide open and alert, the iris a chestnut color near the pupil but with an outer edge as brilliantly scarlet as his father's eyes, and for the first time he began taking an interest in his surroundings. He couldn't see very far because of the density of the forest but everywhere he looked there were nests.

The shabbily constructed platforms, often one beside the other and few separated by more than a foot or so, were on every branch within sight. In the squab's own tree — a fifty-foot beech — there were at least sixty nests below him and a dozen or more above. His own nest was closest to the trunk on this branch and though it was only a short gnarled stub there were five other nests on it, each cradling a squab approximately his own size. The forest was filled with a constant, all-pervading din of peepings from the baby birds.

Twice during each day his parents changed places, but it was not until his tenth day that he took particular notice of its occurrence. It happened in the middle of the morning as he was snuggled under his mother with his head sticking out in wide-eyed curiosity. There came the sound of a great wind and the sky darkened as the entire male population appeared over the forest. With phenomenal agility they swooped into the woods, dodging through thickly interlaced branches and avoiding collision with one another with an incredible skill belied only by the ease with which it was accomplished.

As his father neared the nest from the rear his mother shot off the other side and plummeted earthward. While the larger bird settled over him, his mother swept along close to the ground with a multitude of other females, and not until all the males were out of the air and firmly planted on the nests did they suddenly arrow upwards through the trees and burst into the sky above. Swiftly they were lost from view as they winged toward some distant destination.

Five minutes after arriving, his father fed him, but this time it was no longer the smooth and creamy fluid it had been the first half dozen days, nor even the heavy curded cheese-like material it had become after that. Instead, what little curd was there surrounded fair-sized pieces of harder, only partially transformed natural foods. It was not an unpleasant change for the squab passenger pigeon.

In the middle of the afternoon the change of parents was reenacted, with this time the males darting along near the ground until the females were settled before thrusting themselves up and away. This time, too, the regurgitation of food from his mother's crop was thick with softened acorns and numerous whole beechnuts. Although he ate from her eagerly, it took longer than it had with his father because of a difficulty she seemed to be experiencing.

A faint moaning sound escaped her and she was having considerable trouble in keeping her balance. As she crouched over him, more than the usual amount of her body weight rested upon him and he felt suffocated. When this happened he would push up against her protestingly and the weight would ease off somewhat.

However, before long she would be pressing down upon him again until he peeped and struggled in panic. The discomfort lasted until she fed him a second time, after which she flitted from the nest to the bare branch. Here she perched shakily, fluttering constantly in order to maintain her balance. The reason for her difficulty became apparent. Her right leg, just below the feathers, was shattered and flopped loosely, held to the upper leg only by a thin sliver of the tough pink skin.

Several of her right wing pinion feathers, too, were broken and stuck out weirdly, and as the squab watched with interest she plucked these off with her beak and they spiraled downward.

In another nest only inches behind her, a rather small squab sat upright and peeped plaintively. It was the first time the large leader's squab had seen this adjoining nest unattended and then, as he looked about him, he observed that a number of other nests in this and surrounding trees were devoid of adults and from each of these the pitiful peeping arose.

Even as he watched, no little frightened, a female in one of the nests above him abruptly jumped from her nest and beat her wings frantically as she hovered in one spot. Then, as if punctured by a pin, she collapsed and tumbled limply to the ground where there was a distinct thud as she struck. She didn't move again.

The squab passenger pigeon became even more frightened at that, and he peeped loudly until his mother returned to the nest and settled over him. After that he gave his attention only to the wonderful warmth above him and the chunky but delightfully appeasing food that flooded into his mother's throat and thence into his own mouth.

It was unusually cold that night and the baby bird was in something of a dilemma. If he protested too loudly at his mother's weight, she would hop from the nest and wait a long, cold time before resettling over him, and if he didn't object at all, the pressure of her weight became ever greater upon him until he felt he was being crushed.

It was during those shiftings that night that occasionally he would hear the continued weak peepings from uncovered nestlings. The unknown fear would then rise in him again and only gradually dissipate when the cries were muffled as his mother settled over him.

At dawn, as usual, he was ravenous, but this time there was little food left in her to give him and his hunger was not appeased. He cried out demandingly but, though she took his head in her mouth and her body stiffened spasmodically again and again with her efforts to regurgitate more for him, it was to no avail.

As the sun rose higher and the air warmed considerably, she fluttered in and out of the nest very nervously, and it was during one of these times that her dangling leg caught in the interwoven twigs of the nesting platform and was pulled off. She made no outcry, though it must have pained her, and in fact with the annoyance of the loosely hanging extremity gone, she seemed more sure of herself and calmed down. She rested quietly for a little while until, without a backward glance, she thrust herself into the air and sped away, her flight apparently unhampered either by the loss of the leg or the several missing pinion feathers.

Her flight was observed by other females, who also left their nest, and the air became crowded with them. In a very short time all the females were gone, with the exception of a rather large hen hunched on her nest with her eyes closed in an adjoining beech tree. She seemed not even to have heard the other females leave.

It was the first time that the squabs had been left all alone and it frightened them. An overwhelming chorus of peepings filled the woods and continued unabated for the better part of an hour until the sky darkened with the arrival of the males. But numerous though the males were who came now, their numbers had definitely diminished, and as they settled upon their individual nests it became apparent that a significant number of the little nesting platforms had remained unattended. From these the peepings became even more frantic.

The large leader came in gently, but this time he did not settle over the squab. He alighted instead on the side of the nest, and the little pigeon, now three-fourths the size of his own mother, scrambled awkwardly but with enthusiasm over to his father and plunged his head into the readily opened mouth.

He was very hungry and the fact that there was considerably more solid food being regurgitated for him than curd did not give him pause. He gobbled heartily until his own crop was huge and when his father pulled away and shut his mouth he settled back on his well-rounded stomach and looked about him.

The nest nearest to him was still without an adult bird and the little squab lay stretched out upon it, only very rarely raising its head just a little way off the platform and too weak even to peep.

In the adjoining beech a male that had returned was fluttering perplexedly around his nest, unable to understand why his mate had not departed with the other females and why she did not even acknowledge his presence. She neither moved nor opened her eyes and the male, a younger and smaller bird than the squab's father, appeared to be experiencing increasing distress. At length he alighted on the branch and nudged his mate with his bill, but she was stiff and cold, and not until then did he accept the fact that she was dead and that his squab, if it still lived beneath her, must soon die itself from the weight of her body or from hunger.

Without further hesitation the slender male flew to a nearby nest where an untended squab cried in hunger, and he allowed this fledgling to eat its fill from him. While it might have appeared so, this was not a matter of pity on his part for the plight of the unfed baby; it was merely the most suitable means to relieve the almost unbearable pressure of the food in his crop. When the eager squab had finished feeding, the male flew away silently and did not return again.

An hour later, after his own father had fed him a second time with the little that remained in his crop, the squab passenger pigeon watched this handsome bird join the circling males above the woods, and soon they flew off and the squabs were once more by themselves.

By now the late April air was warm and alive with the sense of spring, and since their appetites were for the moment appeased, the squabs did not protest quite so much at this abandonment. Even before the last of the food they had received from the males was digested, the females returned to feed them again, after which they too left immediately.

This new pattern of feeding and leaving was maintained until the thirteenth day. Five or six times during the day the males came to feed them and then fly off and then the females would do the same at intervals with the males. The food being given to the fledglings now was almost entirely whole — principally acorns and beechnuts, but with a scattering of birch and alder catkins and a few heavily swelled buds from a variety of trees and bushes.

It was during these past few days that a very marked transformation had taken place in the squab. He was now fully feathered and had taken on considerably more of the appearance of the adults. True, his tail and pinion feathers were still awfully short and a sprinkling of the ridiculous-looking yellow filament feathers stuck through the plumage of head and shoulders, but certainly at this stage no one could have mistaken him for anything except a young passenger pigeon.

His color was by no means the same as his father's yet. He

showed no trace of even the buff bluish coloration of his mother, and instead wore a coat that was a uniform brown and which gave no indication of the forthcoming adult plumage coloration. Many of the feathers on his wings and throat were edged with white and these imparted to him an appealing scaled look. But while he was still only twelve inches in total length, he was extremely plump and well outweighed either of his parents.

In one respect only did he differ from the multitude of male squabs in this nesting area. On the forward edge of his right wing, on the joint which coincides with the wrist of a human, there was a patch of feathers the size and shape of a willow leaf which were snow white. When his wings were folded along his sides this peculiarity was visible only as a thin white line, but when his wings were outstretched it became a startling flash of unexpected brilliance visible for a great distance.

Pure albinism was not too uncommon among the passenger pigeons as a species, and partial albinos were even more frequent. This latter condition was normally manifested in a hodge-podge scattering of white feathers throughout the plumage of the bird, giving it a rather mottled effect which wasn't especially attractive. The patch of snow white feathering on the fledgling's wing edge, however, did nothing to detract from his burgeoning handsomeness. It did, in fact, act as a pleasing accent to the rest of his coloration.

Although he made no attempt to leave the nest, he began standing up frequently and exercising his wings exuberantly.

He exulted in the compelling sensation which came as his weight left his feet briefly and he was holding himself aloft with wingpower alone. All during that thirteenth day this incredible nesting area — two miles wide and a full forty-eight miles long — was in a continuous uproar with the exercising of wings by the fledglings.

It was on this day, too, that the fledgling passenger pigeon had watched with longing the powerful flight of his parents as they came and went. Each time they vaulted from the nest and disappeared from sight there grew in him an ever stronger desire to thrust himself away from the outgrown platform and slip through the air with the remarkable speed and effortless grace they exhibited.

Late in the morning of his fourteenth day when both of his parents swooped to the nest simultaneously after an absence of over two hours, he became so excited he nearly tumbled out. All through the great colony both parents were returning to their nests together and, since they had never done this before, the little passenger pigeon squeaked in a comical falsetto imitation of his father's voice and did a sort of skipping dance on the twigs of the nesting platform.

The large leader fed him first while his mother perched on the limb between them and the nest which contained the now ignored body of the little squab. She seemed to have recovered her balance quite well and had no especial difficulty in perching for a short while on one foot. After several minutes, however, she sank to a crouch so that her stomach was braced against the branch.

The food that this handsome male bird now regurgitated into the fledgling passenger pigeon's mouth no longer showed any trace whatever of milk or curd. It consisted wholly of beechnuts which were not even partially digested, as well as a little bit of sandy grit which adhered to them. The youngster took all he had with avidity.

When his own crop was emptied the big male flew to a nearby branch and began preening himself while the female took his place at the nest. As her mouth opened, the squab once again stuck his head far in and accepted an unusually large regurgitation of beechnuts.

He continued swallowing far beyond the limit of a normal feeding and before long his crop was so swollen with food that it unbalanced him and he had to lean forward on it . . . and still the food kept coming. At length, the last of her crop's contents gone into this offspring, the female bounced lightly back to her own perch and busied herself preening her breast feathers.

Despite the female's loss of a leg and a few of her wing feathers, she and the large male made a most handsome pair. The demands of their greedy squab during this nesting period had caused both of them to lose a good bit of their body weight and, compared with their slender streamlined bearings, the fledgling passenger pigeon was now a very curious sight.

His crop, extending much beyond its normal swollen limits, was enormous and very nearly equaled the size of his entire body. In fact he looked uncommonly like a bird with a single head and two bodies, and he was so lethargic as a result of this feeding that a sort of stupor overcame him and he could do little more than lie upon the twig platform and blink.

This greed on the squab's part was matched by that of those everywhere in this extensive nursery. Sated far beyond anything they had ever experienced before, the squabs lay quietly, as if drugged. With the noon hour close, a rare silence grew in the woods.

His mother joined his father on the stub of a branch just above him and their heads touched together tenderly for a little while. Soon even this activity ceased and they sat quiescent but alert, their elegant bodies poised as if containing tightly coiled springs only awaiting a signal to be released and catapult the birds away.

It was his father who started this signal. After looking at his squab for a long quiet moment, the large leader uttered a low soothing note and then raised his head high and screeched piercingly. An identical note was echoed immediately from a thousand, ten thousand, a hundred thousand males and more throughout the vast nesting colony, and in that instant the entire population of adults thundered skyward, climbed to a great height before leveling off and swiftly became a heavy gray cloud disappearing to the northeast.

That was the last time the fledgling passenger pigeon saw his parents.

3

THE fledgling passenger pigeon occupied himself during that first couple of hours alone by merely dozing or gazing about him. Although it was odd to see these woods wholly devoid of adult birds for so long, it did not immediately concern him. His crop was filled to bursting with the most delicious food he had ever eaten, and he was perfectly content to lie there and observe his surroundings as the beechnuts digested.

After three hours, however, when his crop had reduced in size by an eighth, a certain nervousness became evident in him. His parents had never stayed away so long before and even the presence of many hundreds of squabs his own size within sight did not ease the growing loneliness tinged with fear.

During the next hour he scrambled about his nest, often flapping his wings vigorously and scanning the skies above, but more frequently toddling to the very brink of the nest and teetering there precariously.

Six feet away and as many feet below him was another branch somewhat larger than his own. Even though it had four nests upon it, there was plenty of bare branch upon which to alight and there could be no doubt that he was contemplating trying out his wings in a little flight to this station. The longer he studied it, the more attainable it seemed.

The bright little line of white on his right wrist area spread and flashed as he opened his wings and began flapping them. The wingbeats were rather slow at first and decidedly awkward, but gradually their action smoothed and coordinated and picked up speed until they were a blur above him. Before he even realized what was happening, he was airborne and his nest was several feet behind him.

Instead of exhilaration, however, he was swept by an awful fear and became panicky. The ground was dreadfully far below and somehow his wings simply were not functioning as they should. Already, in just these few seconds, they were tiring alarmingly of holding his excessive weight aloft and he began losing altitude.

He missed the branch he was aiming for by a foot or more but managed to slam into the bouncy slender end of another branch some eight feet below that. His feet gripped desperately but to no avail because, though they caught hold well enough, the branch was too willowy and bent sharply beneath him, dumping him once more into open air.

About a dozen feet farther down was a very large branch, and so he angled toward it and struck with such force that the breath wheezed from his mouth and he almost tumbled off. Only with the most determined of flapping and scrambling was he able to maintain his perch and even then his balance was so unsteady that he continued to dip back and forth precariously for several seconds before being able to crouch on the wide limb and hold himself reasonably straight.

The branch on which he perched and the ground beneath him were thickly spattered with crusted droppings, and at many places directly below nests these deposits of guano were built up in mounds as much as a foot in depth.

The forest, which from his nest had seemed so close and friendly, was now a huge, alien and definitely frightening place. He cocked an eye upward but knew without attempting it that he could not hope to reach the abandoned nest many feet above him and so, for a time, he merely crouched on the thick branch and trembled with a rather pleasant combination of fear and excitement.

Another squab fluttered past him, its wings beating furiously. It, too, hit the large branch but was unable to keep its balance, slipped off and plopped to the ground fifteen feet below. The ground cover was spongy here and the bird bounced a little, then got its feet situated beneath it and crouched, a bit dazed but seemingly unhurt.

The fledgling passenger pigeon's daring little flight had caused something of a chain reaction, for now other squabs were fluttering out of their nests all over the forest. In the majority of cases these attempts at first flight were pathetic. A good many of the birds missed the first limb aimed for and cartwheeled all the way down to the ground. For quite some time the woods were filled with the sound of an orchard in a strong wind with apples abundantly thumping to the ground.

A certain percentage of the squabs were injured in their falls, but usually the beating of their wings slowed them enough so that little more damage was done than a bit of wind knocked out. With sunset still some hours away, the ground was already heavily strewn with squabs squatting disconsolately and no little nervous at their predicament.

In the beech tree, the white patch on the squab's wing flashed brightly as once again he assayed this business of flight. This time he showed some improvement, angling to the ground a full thirty feet away after narrowly missing collision with a sapling. Upon arrival at the earth, however, he found himself unable to check his speed properly, and he slammed headlong into another squab. The two of them tumbled over in the dead leaves, each squeaking protestingly at the other.

An unusually frenzied flapping caught his attention and he looked up. Several feet above him a fat female squab had jammed herself inextricably in the first crotch of a sapling and struggled helplessly, her strength fast fading. She was, he quickly noted, only one of numerous squabs so ensnared. Some managed to pull themselves free only slightly injured but others were much less fortunate. Only a dozen feet away from him and less than a foot off the ground a fine little male jerked spasmodically, his throat tightly wedged in the springy V of a low branch. As he watched, the struggles ceased and the bird's body went limp.

By the end of another half-hour, few squabs remained on their platforms, and throughout the length and breadth of the great nesting area the ground was literally alive with fledglings. Many of them hunched stupidly where they had alighted, dumbfounded at their new location and unable to comprehend why their parents did not return.

Others bumbled about drunkenly, frequently collapsing in heaps as their weak legs gave out under the unaccustomed strain of walking. Still others persevered in their attempts to fly, and though they drummed their wings with the greatest of exertion, they were unable to raise their fat bodies more than a foot into the air before falling back in exhaustion.

The woodland had become a vast circus in which the squabs played the leading roles as clowns, their endeavors at walking and flying made even more humorous by the seriousness with which they were attempted.

The world here on the forest floor was amazingly different from that on the nesting platforms, and the fledgling passenger pigeon delighted in the sensations he was experiencing. The moist cover of leaves sank slightly under his weight and everything looked and smelled intriguing. Although he wanted to explore, the weight and bulkiness of his still grossly swollen crop hampered his movements and tired him, and he had to stop often to rest. At such times he leaned heavily against the ground because it was too much of an effort to hold the crop erect. The posture this caused was laughable, for with the huge crop almost buried in leaves his little tail and rump were projected upward and it looked as if he were trying to stand on his head.

In addition to the prevailing din of flapping wings and

rustling of debris on the forest floor, there was a raucous and constant wailing from the squabs. The fledgling found himself making this same new sound: a high-pitched sort of cackling uttered as if the birds were short of breath which, in most cases, they were.

What humor existed in the actions of these squabs did not long remain. The en masse departure of the adult passenger pigeons from the nesting area had not gone unnoticed. From all over in a great radius around these woods there came a convergence of a variety of creatures: foxes and wolves, hawks and eagles, crows and buzzards and owls, all approaching openly, brazenly, loping across open fields and skimming through the late afternoon air.

Slinking through the forest depths came others. There were bobcats, cougars and lynxes, bears and raccoons, opossums and skunks and the most deadly of the four-legged killers, the martens, weasels and mink and even a few wolverines.

The first indication of danger came to the fledgling as he waddled about aimlessly still within sight of his own beech tree, jostled by the multitude of his equally unsteady fellows. The attack took him by complete surprise.

There was a sudden flurry of activity to his right, and abruptly he was bowled over by a wave of squabs scattering in abject panic. As he struggled upright again, the reason for this behavior became horribly clear.

Only ten feet away a huge goshawk, fully four times as large as he, stood over the body of a weakly struggling squab, holding it down with one viciously taloned foot. The hawk's eyes glittered fiercely as it swiveled its head back and forth several times, and then it fell to feeding. The cruelly hooked beak ripped into the little bird's soft distended belly and pulled loose a mass of entrails which it immediately swallowed. A great chunk of breast meat was pulled away and devoured next, and that was all the fledgling passenger pigeon saw, for now he too fled in blind panic from this awesome predator.

Hawks of all kinds — even a few gigantic bald eagles — wheeled low over the forest and screamed in joyful anticipation before plunging through the treetops to grasp the grounded squabs and devour them. The little pigeon hawks were there, too, and the duck hawks; the small but deadly sharp-shinned hawks and the ferocious Cooper's hawks. Even a number of the large and relatively slow-flying red-tailed hawks — rodent eaters, principally — could not pass up such a feast as this.

Few of these birds of prey carried squabs away initially, content to gorge themselves on the helpless birds wherever they nailed them. But, as appetites became sated, each rose ponderously on great wings and carried away to its own young the weakly struggling form of a squab.

Twice in succession the fledgling narrowly missed being caught as fledglings around him were pounced upon and impaled, and he continued his panicky scrambling run until finally he crumpled in exhaustion and lay gasping beside a massive moss-covered log. And, surprisingly, despite the fear and noise, his eyes closed and he slept.

It was dusk when he awakened, and his body was all but hidden by the loose leaves which had been blown against the log by the continuous flapping of the squabs as he slept. Now an uneasy near-silence prevailed. The log blocked his view to the left, but to his right he could see that the baby birds had clustered together in individual dense circles thirty or forty feet in diameter, huddling in this manner for warmth and companionship and safety. Unfortunately, it was not the first time for passenger pigeons that the maxim of safety in numbers failed to hold true.

Just as the fledgling was ready to shake free of the leaves and waddle over to the apparent security of the nearest group, a low hissing growl from atop the log froze him in place. Suddenly a slender, two-foot long animal, dark brown above with pale belly fur, leaped over him and in two swift bounds was in the midst of the nearest circle of birds, slashing with an unbelievable frenzy.

It was a New York weasel, and if its speed was incredible, its devastation among the squabs was petrifying. It wasted no time at first in eating but quickly leaped from bird to bird, expertly biting through the skull of each and then dropping it.

A weird and heart-stopping snarl that was a hideous combination of scream and hiss came almost constantly from the bloody mouth of the animal, and the squabs were in a confused uproar. Some of those along the fringe of the circle fled into the gathering darkness, but mostly they milled about defenselessly while this killer whirled and slew with wanton abandon.

[41]

Within fifteen minutes the circle of birds had broken entirely and, while the majority had escaped, there were over a hundred dead birds in a radius of fifty feet. And now, breathing heavily from his exertions, the weasel fed. At bird after bird he paused only long enough to tear open the head and eat the brains, but even his amazing appetite was sated long before the greater portion of dead birds was further touched.

For a long moment the weasel stood high on his hind legs, listening carefully. Satisfied he was in no danger, he commenced scrubbing away the traces of his slaughter. With rapid flicks of his pink tongue he cleaned his feet and then used them to briskly erase the residue of blood from his muzzle and chest fur. A moment longer he paused listening, then dropped to all fours and disappeared with a queer humping lope into the shadows.

The passenger pigeon fledgling remained hidden, still frozen into immobility at the insane fury of this beast. No longer was he tempted to join one of these circular clusters of squabs, although in reality this was not so much through concern lest such an attack be repeated as it was due to the fact that it was now fully dark and his immediate area in the woods was barren of living birds.

His sleep that night was fitful, and many times he was awakened by the sounds of distant fluttering and screeching and the unfamiliar but nonetheless fearsome growls, yaps, roars and hootings of the night feeders. Three separate times when he awoke the pale moonlight illuminated animals he had not seen before. The first time it was a large cat with mottled brown-gray fur and stubby tail sniffing among the circle of dead birds. It batted playfully at one and tossed another high into the air, then pounced upon it when it fell, but it ate nothing and soon drifted away silently.

Another time a fox trotted to the edge of the circle, daintily picked up a bird and carried it away. The final time it was a peculiar and forbidding snapping sound which awakened him and he saw three light-gray animals, with long muzzles and naked tails and ears, crouched among the dead birds. The snapping sound was the crushing of fragile bones as they ate their fill. They took their time about it, and when finally they left, two of this trio of opossums carried squabs away with them.

Even with the arrival of dawn the fledgling passenger pigeon remained hidden. Nor did he move until a great mass of squabs swarmed around his log moving generally eastward and he shook off his fear and joined them.

The terror of the night behind them, the squabs were unconcerned about the occasional carcasses lying about on the ground, and their demeanor reflected nothing more than peace and pleasant curiosity at all they saw. It is one of nature's greatest gifts to her lesser creatures that they neither worry for long about past tragedies nor contemplate to any appreciable degree possible misfortune in the future.

The size of his crop having reduced by half since yesterday, the fledgling found walking not so difficult a matter this morning. His legs were stronger and his pace was more assured. Determined attempts at flight, however, were no more fruitful than yesterday's had been, and after a few vigorous experiments he settled down to being grounded for at least a while longer.

Wherever they went the ground surface was coated with guano and, though it emanated a peculiar pungent odor, it was not offensive to him except that when he encountered the higher piles it frequently caused stumbling. The softness of the dead leaves and occasional patches of brilliant green moss were pleasant to walk upon. All over on the surface leaves and among them there was an abundance of beechnuts and acorns, for the parent birds had never fed in the nesting area or its vicinity, but the fledgling paid little attention to them now.

The phenomenal number of squabs here gave little indication of depletion through the concerted attacks by predators throughout the night. Actually, except for scatterings of dead birds or the remains of them here and there, the squabs appeared as populous as ever.

That the desire to fly burned brightly in them all was apparent when every few minutes great segments of this marching throng would flap vigorously and skitter along an inch or so above the ground for a few yards, making up in great enthusiasm what they lacked in skill. Such attempts at flight invariably wound up in a huge pile-up punctuated by a sort of chagrined clucking as they extricated themselves from the tangle of wings and legs and bodies and continued their walking.

From far to the south of them came a barely audible but rather disturbing sound. It was a high rumbling which continued for a considerable while until, just as the birds had become accustomed to it, it ceased and was replaced by even stranger noises: sharp cracking sounds, similar to but not quite the same as the breaking of branches, and vague shoutings. As a constant background to this came the murmur of countless wings beating ceaselessly, as if a brisk wind blew through a forest of autumn-dry leaves.

Disturbing though these sounds were, they were remote and there was no evidence of possible danger to themselves, so the squabs continued unchecked in their exploration. And soon even that vague disturbance was forgotten in the wonder of discovering all these fascinating new things.

The morning had become bright and unusually warm and the sun was relatively high when this leading segment of the march in which the fledgling waddled abruptly crossed into a section of woods where there was no longer a heavy guano deposit on the ground and no nesting platforms cluttered the trees above them.

These trees were much more fully budded than those behind and for the first time he saw birds smaller than himself — tiny black-capped chickadees flitting from branch to branch; here a sooty-gray titmouse, its crest held pertly erect as it stared curiously at this odd blanket of walking birds; there a pair of speckled black-and-white downy woodpeckers, one with a bright red patch at the back of his head, both of them clinging expertly to the stub of a dead birch and drumming industriously; in a low bush a sleek, olive-colored cedar waxwing, its bright eyes encased in a rakish black mask and its topknot comically raising and lowering. There were sparrows, too, and blue jays, and from beside a rotted stump a large rabbit rose on its hind legs, twitched its nose a few times toward the advancing assemblage and then casually hopped off into the undergrowth.

Each different newly sprouted plant was investigated closely, and at one spot near a scraggly little cedar tree the fledgling passenger pigeon stood for five minutes watching a beetle move sluggishly through the leaves.

Gradually he had been working his way toward the van of this eastward movement, and while his frequent stops to study tiny ferns and wildflowers and twigs and other fascinating things slowed him to some extent, it slowed the others as well. Still, it was mid-afternoon by the time he shoved his way into the leading edge of the now very slowly moving division of birds. Here he paused momentarily on a little hillock to look around.

Ahead the woods was considerably brighter and behind him the blanket of squabs stretched out endlessly. He stepped down, tripped, rolled completely over and regained his feet, then struck out for the lighter area ahead at a good pace.

In another fifteen minutes, having moved along slightly faster than the rest of the line, the fledgling found himself at a sort of spearhead of the flock, a few thousand squabs extending ahead of the others to a tapering point perhaps fifty yards in advance of the main body.

The unusual noises to the south had continued without pause and now were definitely louder. Having become accustomed to the sound over a period of hours, however, the squabs remained unafraid. The meandering movement toward the east continued, and quite surprisingly the trees ended and the edge of the forest stretched to north and south as far as the fledgling could see.

Running parallel to the edge of this woods was a peculiar bare stretch of ground a dozen or more feet wide and very straight. Here the earth was solidly packed, devoid of growth. Running the length of it was a pair of great ruts, often over a foot deep.

On the other side of this packed earth was a vast open field of brown stubble, and since the fledgling had never before seen ground barren of trees he eyed it suspiciously. He would have turned back now to reenter the woods, but the mass of birds still coming from behind forced him farther into the open. With difficulty he scrambled across the deep ruts and beyond them into the stubble field. On and on he was forced, and when finally the flock did come to a halt it was not until he was fully seventy yards out in this field.

While many of the young birds, wearied by their exertions, simply crouched down where they were and dozed unconcernedly, the fledgling passenger pigeon felt instinctively nervous at being in the open like this and began to swing his lead point around in a wide southwest curve back toward the woods.

With no trees at all to mute the noises here, the sounds they had been hearing all day came to them very clearly and at least part of the mystery of their origin was resolved. Far down the road was a long line of dozens of wagons and a great number of men. Perplexed at such a strange sight, the pigeons stopped and watched as a regular procession of more of the two-legged creatures emerged from the woods carrying large baskets and sacks, the contents of which were tumbled into the wagon beds.

In just a short while the leading eight wagons came to life and commenced rolling along the road toward them, their teams straining in their traces. There came a heavy rumble from these wagons, similar in quality to the rumble heard early that morning by the birds but now definitely lower in tone and with less rattling.

As these wagons neared them the fledgling passenger pigeon sensed some sort of menace and crouched quietly in the stubble. His movement caused a similar reaction in the entire leading portion of the flock, all the way around the bend of the march and back to the road.

In the distance more men had come from the woods and emptied their loads, and their wagons also started north. As the first one of the eight that had begun the procession approached the area where the squabs were thickly covering the road for over three hundred yards, the men began shouting back and forth excitedly.

"By golly, look up ahead there!" cried the first teamster, pointing at the squabs watching their approach with more curiosity than fear.

"Sure looks like we been wasting our time clawing through the woods after 'em," replied a burly, bearded man walking with a group of others at the rear of the lead wagon. "Just our stupid luck not to see 'em in the open like this until after all the wagons are plumb full." He spat a long stream of brown liquid onto the road.

Now that they were closer it could be seen that each of these wagons had boarded sides several feet in height and inside each, mounded like grain in the wagon beds, were the carcasses of squabs. As these conveyances lurched and bumped along the rutted road, many of the dead birds were thrown off, and it was the job of the young boys walking alongside the wagon train to retrieve those that fell and toss them back onto the piles.

When the lead wagon reached a point a dozen yards in front of the birds, its driver hollered "Whoah!" and then removed his hat and mopped his brow when the wagon stopped.

"Don't recollect ever seeing 'em this thick on the road before." He shook his head and squinted at the birds. "Well, we can't afford to pass up an opportunity like this, so it looks like our work ain't done yet today after all. Pass the word back, Sam. Just the driver and one walking boy with each wagon. The rest'll stay here and pile 'em up until we can unload and come back from town."

"My gawd, George," protested the bearded man, "we been at it all day. I'm tired. So're the others. Let's just come back for 'em again tomorrow."

The lead driver shook his head. "See that curve?" He pointed out in the stubble field toward the fledgling. "They're turning already to go back into the woods. We ain't gonna get 'em this easy later on. Anyway, they ain't gonna be on the ground much longer. Maybe by tomorrow they'll be starting to fly. We gotta get 'em now. Now do like I say and pass the word."

The bigger man grumbled but cupped his hands and shouted to the men along the line of stopped wagons. Within a few minutes over two hundred men and boys had gathered off the road, and the wagon train lurched forward again.

The man called George stood up and called back to them, "We'll dump these and be back with some empty wagons about dark. Now don't be fooling around. You work at it, might be we'll double the day's take. Just remember, every bird is worth six cents!"

The teams snorted nervously as they were forced into the flock of birds but the drivers laid on with their whips and there was no choice for them. Each time a hoof of one of these great dray horses thudded to the ground one or two squabs was killed. Worse by far, however, was the destruction in the deep ruts. Here the pigeons were two or three birds deep in many places and, while some of those on the top layer managed to scramble out of harm's way, hundreds of birds were crushed beneath the wide metal rims of the heavy-laden wheels. This made for difficult driving, and the teamsters cursed these miserable, ignorant birds that made their job harder.

Even while the wagons were still passing, the men and boys set to work and the slaughter commenced. They waded into the midst of the heaviest concentration of birds and worked swiftly with no time taken even for conversation.

Their method was mechanical, efficient and very brutal. Walking in a sort of half crouch, a man's hand would dart out, grasp a squab across the back, pinning its wings to its sides, and pick it up. The other hand, with first and second fingers spread in a V, would catch the bird just below the swollen crop. With a quick snap, both head and crop were ripped off and the carcass, flapping and kicking, was dropped. There was a good reason for removing the crop with the head; birds lying dead with their crops still attached tended to spoil much more quickly.

Behind the men came boys with wicker baskets to pick up the birds that had been thus "cleaned." When their baskets were full they were carried to a central location and dumped. The pile of dead birds grew with awful speed, and the fledgling passenger pigeon crouched even lower in the stubble.

While the onslaught by these men had begun in the field and road, it now swung toward the woods as the birds flew clumsily in that direction. It was no great task to keep pace with the heaviest concentrations of the birds and continue the grisly work.

The very density of their numbers hampered the squabs in their flight, and progress back into the woods was painfully slow. The pile of carcasses grew constantly higher and broader until finally, in the fading sunlight, a stream of wagons appeared far up the road and a relieved cry went up from the workers. They straightened, arching their backs to ease the pain caused by this constant crouching, then sauntered back to the mass of dead birds just off the road.

The boys, free for a little while from their chores, now gathered at the edge of the woods, where they found wind-downed branches which they broke to suitable size and then amused themselves with a macabre sort of golf game in which the upraised heads of the squabs still crouched in the stubble were the "balls."

Usually a swat from such a stick merely crushed the skull, but occasionally the bird's head would be knocked clean from the body and whiz through the air like a stone, making an odd whirring sound, and such an accomplishment brought cries of delight from the youngsters.

A group of eight of these stick-wielders worked their way toward the fledgling passenger pigeon in the leading edge of the curve, and the dreadful sound of their weapons hissing through the air and thumping into the birds so unnerved him him that he abruptly burst to his feet and began a queer, wing-flopping run toward the woods.

Instantly the uninjured birds behind him followed his lead, and there was a veritable wave of movement as more birds than the men realized were still there arose from the stubble and surged forward.

The men roared with laughter as the entire band of boys took up the pursuit, screeching wildly as Indians and swinging their clubs with abandon, striking the birds anywhere they could. This fine game would undoubtedly have taken many more of the squabs' lives had not one of the youths been whacked soundly across the bridge of his nose by a companion's wild swing. The cartilage was crushed, and he tumbled in a screaming heap on the ground as bright red blood gushed through the fingers clasped over his face.

That ended all fun and games in an instant and as the boys crowded around awkwardly and sympathetically, the remainder of this contingent of squabs thundered into the comparative safety of the darkening woods.

The birds kept going long after they were out of immediate danger and the sounds of the loading back at the road came only dimly to them. And when finally they stopped and huddled together weak and forlorn, the trees above them once again filled with nesting platforms, it was full dark. For these squabs, the first day out of the nest had been a tragic one indeed.

Back at the road the work of loading the wagons was finally ending. Not enough wagons had returned for all the birds that had been slain and so a rather large pile of headless and cropless squabs was left behind. The chief hunter cursed thickly at this, not because of the wastefulness of having killed far more birds than necessary, but because of the loss of money it meant. The lives of these birds were meaningless to him in any other terms. There had always been billions of passenger pigeons and there always would be, and he would continue in years to come, as he had in years past, to make a tidy little fortune each spring with his shipments of hundreds of barrels of squabs to Chicago and Detroit, Cleveland and elsewhere.

This was, unfortunately, the same attitude held by hundreds, even thousands, of other men who annually engaged in the same pursuit throughout the passenger pigeon's nesting range from Minnesota to Maine and from western Kentucky to Delaware.

Most of these men had heard about — and even laughed over — the damning account of their activities that had been published a few years back in *The Chicago Field*. In this publication Professor H. B. Roney of Saginaw had written in considerable detail about the atrocious annual destruction of the passenger pigeons.

He wrote about one pigeon slaughter in particular which had occurred a little more than a hundred miles north of this site near the city of Petosky less than a decade ago. A great nesting had taken place there which had attracted pigeon hunters, trappers and netters from all over, and the carnage had been so great that it simply staggered the imagination.

Roney very carefully estimated the number of birds that had been killed at that nesting and the total — including the tens of thousands that were shipped away alive and the hundreds of thousands left behind, dead or dying — was no less than *one billion* birds!

He may have exaggerated a little, though certainly not much, but his arguments, to quote his adversaries, had backfired in his own face. Instead of decreasing, as he had predicted, the birds were apparently more numerous than ever — as this flock right here very plainly indicated. It would take a thousand years to even make a dent in populations like that.

And so these hunters near Big Rapids cared not one whit that they had killed an astounding number of birds despite the fact that only two hundred men had been engaged in the day's work. What they had taken — and wasted — was only a small fraction of the total population. And yet, on this single day in Newaygo County, Michigan, almost a quarter of a million squabs had been slain.

4

SEVEN days after leaving his nest, the young passenger pigeon had found his wings and was in good flying condition. It had been an eventful and extremely hectic week, but not again quite so fraught with disaster as had been the first day.

For three days he had been unable to fly, and even though his crop had become empty by the second morning it was not until the day after that, when much of the heavy layer of fat on his body had been used up and the sharp pangs of hunger stabbed him, that he finally began to eat on his own.

The beechnuts and acorns which he had at first ignored were now sought eagerly among the leaves, and though there was a considerable abundance of them they didn't last long among the greedy squabs. He burned up a great deal of energy just seeking the food along with the other fledglings, and he was unable to get his crop even more than half full. It quickly became necessary to range farther and farther each day for food.

By the end of five days on the ground his wing feathers were well developed, but his tail was still so short as to make him rudderless and awkward in flight. The great army of fledglings had now more or less formed into smaller groupings of several hundred birds each, and it bordered on the hilarious to watch their attempts at flight.

It would begin with a wild wing-flapping on the ground and a scrambling run, and suddenly they would be flying two or three feet off the ground. Unable to maneuver well because of the lack of tail, they would have to swerve widely and far in advance in order to miss trees and other obstructions. Even then some of the birds damaged themselves by slamming into branches.

Landing was the most difficult and, except to the fledglings themselves, the most amusing. With no fan-like tail feathers to flare and act as a brake to their speed and still unable to estimate distances very well, the flock would grow tired after a flight of half a mile or so and angle to the ground. The initial pile-ups as they landed were like groups of children piling together after a football. As they touched the ground they would pitch head over heels in an awful tangle, and even after pulling themselves apart and sitting upright they would appear to be dumfounded at what had happened.

Now, however, on the seventh day, the young passenger pigeon became more sure of himself in flight. He was able to fly considerable distances without rest, and even though he was yet far from graceful in his maneuverings, he was nonetheless able to turn with reasonable accuracy and land with a certain degree of stability.

And it was now, with his own little flock of two hundred, that the young passenger pigeon left this nesting area behind for good. These woods had become far too hazardous a place to remain. The continued onslaught of men and animal predators had taken a frightful toll of the birds this week, but while he had experienced close calls on several occasions with hawks and once with a lynx, he had managed to stay clear of the most dreaded foe, man.

Others hadn't been so fortunate. Every day the men were there, chasing, clubbing, shooting at them, but after that initial disastrous encounter the young passenger pigeon's band had moved ever farther from the road, whence these men always seemed to come.

They flew low when they left, heading generally northward. They seldom rose much higher than twelve feet, still somewhat afraid of sustained flight at considerable altitudes. As a result their flying was not the arrow-straight process of the adults but rather a slow, meandering hopping across the countryside. They stayed mainly over what open ground they could find, curving wide to miss individual tall trees or woods. Whenever a stream angled in their direction they followed it, curving wherever the stream bed curved and often flying twice as far as an adult might have flown to cover the same distance.

To the young passenger pigeon flying was a wonderful experience. The thrill of the air hissing past, the constantly changing panorama below, the growing power of his wings and continuously improving maneuverability filled him with a sense of exultation such as he had never known. Never again would he depend upon his inadequate legs to carry him to safety.

They stopped frequently to eat and drink and bathe. There was an abundance of food everywhere now. A good supply of beechnuts still littered the forest floors and even the acorns remained in reasonable supply, but there was much else to eat.

The fields were now alive with new greenery, the trees filled with leaves. Early wild strawberries were forming, and under every cluster of dead leaves there were crickets and slugs, snails and earthworms and a variety of insects delightful to the palate.

One of the most exciting finds, a few weeks after leaving the nesting area, was a salt deposit. The young birds had been attracted to it by rather extensive flocks of adult passenger pigeons alighting at the spot. While these adults showed no objection to the young birds' landing here, neither did they display any particular desire to have them join their roost some miles distant, and so the young birds continued to roost by themselves in a clump of hemlocks.

The salt deposit was along a little creek and it was in both thin slabs and loose crystals mixed with the earth from which it projected. At first the young passenger pigeon eyed it with suspicion because it looked like no foodstuff he had ever seen before, but since the adults were gobbling it greedily he tried it, too, and delighted in its wonderful taste. Soon he and his entire flock were eating it every bit as avidly as the adults, pausing only now and then to flutter or waddle to the creek to drink deeply and then play in the shallow water, splashing with their wings and having a generally good time.

Except for their shorter tails and the overall brownish coloration of their plumage, the young differed very little from the adults. The graceful head, long neck and streamlined body were the same, now that the fledgling fat had been used up, and even their tailfeathers were growing rapidly and would soon be as long and as important to their flight as were those of the adults.

They stayed at the salt deposit area for more than a week, ranging far over the countryside in their little band for food, but always coming back to the hemlock roost in this vicinity. On three different occasions the young passenger pigeon had tried to join one of the adult flocks, but they had little concern for him. When they took off it was with great speed. They climbed high and hurtled through the air so fast that he was quickly left behind and so he always returned to his own group at the spring.

They would have remained in the area longer, but on the morning of the ninth day a larger flock of perhaps three hundred adults whizzed past them as they winged toward the salt deposit. As these adult birds cupped their wings and began to settle to the ground there came a number of loud explosions. Screeching in alarm, the adults turned to flee. Even more explosions came now as a dozen or more men stepped into the open and continued firing their shotguns.

The adults had been close together in order to land in this little salt deposit clearing and now their bodies tumbled to the earth in great numbers. Scores of them fell lifelessly, and others, wounded and unable to keep up with those unhurt, began coming down at intervals.

The young passenger pigeon himself had screeched a warning as the guns opened up, and though his flock had flared quickly they were too close, and guns were pointed in their direction and fired. Five of the birds close to him collapsed and fell, and a burning pain blossomed in his own right side as a lead pellet creased him. Without breaking the skin it tore away a little furrow of feathers, and for the first time he led his flock quite high, climbing to over one thousand feet and then speeding northward as rapidly as their young wings could carry them.

Only after they were many miles from the ambush did they spiral earthward toward a large stand of birches with a clear rivulet running through them. Once, twice, three times they circled over the area until the young leader was sure it was safe and then they came to rest in the branches.

For a short while they remained tense, their muscles bunched for immediate flight at the first indication of danger, but it quickly became obvious that they were safe here and they relaxed. Thirst was their first concern and they dropped through the branches to the tiny stream and lined up along the bank as they drank their fill of the icy water.

Wormlike catkins clung to a patch of alder scrub along the bank and the young leader plucked one, swallowed it and found it tasty. He was very hungry, as were the others, and soon all of them were hopping from branch to branch in the birches as well as the alders, plucking every catkin within reach and swallowing it.

After eating they dozed for an hour, and when they took off toward the north again they ignored the four birds which huddled injured and dying from buckshot wounds. They flew casually at a height of five hundred feet, for now that he had experienced relatively high flying, the young passenger pigeon was enthralled with it. At this height he felt safe and sure of himself and the forest and fields below were pleasing to the eye.

His sight was extremely keen, and scanning the ground a quarter-mile ahead of them as they flew he was able to see minute things. Over there in that open field a harvest mouse scuttled across a narrow rabbit path. To the right, a noisy flock of newly arrived redwinged blackbirds were arguing melodiously over possession rights for a small marshy area filled with dry cattail reeds near a pond. A mile ahead a hound trotted nonchalantly down the middle of a dusty road, and ten miles ahead the uppermost roofs and spires of a town showed above the trees.

Already becoming wise to the treacherous ways of man, the young passenger pigeon turned slightly to the west and skirted the town of Manton. A few miles beyond this a fine stand of hemlock heavy with new seeds caught his eye, and after several passes the flock alighted and fed again.

They had no particular destination and there was no hurry, so the days passed quickly as they meandered ever northward into the less populated forest country of Michigan's northern Lower Peninsula. Frequently they saw — and often joined for an hour or a day or a week — other flocks of young passengers and even adult birds now and then. But the young passenger had become very leery of towns and roads and buildings, and when the flock they had joined flew directly toward such landmarks, he would angle away and his own contingent would follow.

They traced the eastern shoreline of Grand Traverse Bay's

East Arm, crossed the mile-wide inlet at Elk Rapids and swung in a long northeastward curve over the upper Lake Michigan shoreline past Charlevoix and Bayshore and Petosky.

Just north of Petosky they met and joined a long winding ribbon of mixed adult and juvenile passenger pigeons. Several hundred yards wide, the flock stretched behind for six miles, and almost six and a half million birds flew here.

It was the young passenger pigeon's first flight in such a large flock and he reveled in the sensation. The thunder of the wings was a soothing music to his ears and, since his flock had joined close to the rear, he was delighted with the way the passage of the birds created a wind of its own and helped pull him along so that it was a less difficult task to keep up with the adults.

The fact that they apparently had some definite destination excited him too. He was content to remain far back with his little band, and though miles ahead he could see the leading point of the column turning in a great curve to the right he made no attempt to shorten the distance by flying a diagonal line toward it.

The landscape below was filled with lakes of all sizes and shapes and the forests surrounding them were mostly unbroken. Houses were very few, and cleared fields scarce. The air was crisp and cool and smelled freshly washed by the waters of Lake Michigan to their left and Lake Huron to their right.

The flock was still a dozen miles south of the Straits of Mackinac when, from high and to one side, a large male peregrine falcon bulleted down in a screaming dive into a dense section of the flock only a hundred yards behind the leaders.

Instantly the wings of the birds at this point made sharp cracking sounds as they dropped and veered severely to escape the predator, and all but one of them did. The single bird was struck a frightful blow by the half-closed "fist" of the hawk. There was an explosion of feathers as he hit it, and the pigeon tumbled lifelessly to the ground while the falcon followed it closely in a steep spiral.

The danger was gone for the moment but a noteworthy phenomenon was now taking place in the flock. As the column of birds continued forward, they dropped and veered sharply upon reaching the exact spot where the bird of prey had attacked, perfectly emulating the movement of that portion of the flock which had been there when it happened. And so, instead of a level, if wavering, line of flight from front to rear, there was a great dip, curve and recovery to the original line of flight. It gave the queer illusion of the flock hanging motionless while this deeply undulating ripple traversed the length of the column.

As far back as he had been, the young passenger pigeon was of course unaware that the attack had occurred, but as he neared the point where far below on the ground a peregrine falcon had already almost completed its meal, he saw the bird in front of him drop and veer, and a wingbeat later, at the precise spot, he did the same. In a moment he had followed the bird ahead as it swiftly reascended to join the main column.

It was not the last time this was to happen on the flight, nor was such a maneuver always the result of an attempt to avoid danger. Now and then the leaders would turn sharply left or right, and with the precision of a drill team on parade each of the birds following would turn in precisely the same way at exactly the same spot.

A spirit of playfulness appeared to take hold of the leaders as they crossed over the five-mile-wide Mackinac Strait. From a height of some seven hundred feet they swung around in a sharp, prolonged curve. In moments they had formed a loop in the column and passed thirty feet or so beneath it. The curve persisted and the leaders descended ever lower in this huge spiral. Not until they were only twenty feet above the choppy waters did they level off and head north again.

The result of this action was astonishing. For fully five minutes, as the entire column followed this exact maneuver, there appeared to be a gigantic coil spring positioned in the sky. With simply dropping a short distance, the young passenger pigeon could easily have rejoined the column a hundred yards or even a half mile ahead, but though he saw the birds below him he did not break the pattern, nor did any of the others.

Over the last mile of open water before reaching the pine-cloaked slopes of the Upper Peninsula, the leaders maneuvered in a series of curves, loops and even sharp-angled turns. They flew with a great joy and gusto, as if delighting in the power of their wings and in the wonders of flight. When the shore was less than a quarter-mile ahead, the inspiring coil formation was formed again but this time in reverse as the leaders circled ever higher until they had regained their former altitude.

Across the Upper Peninsula counties of Mackinac and Chippewa they flew, arrowing their dense column over the Sault Sainte Marie and into the sky over the lake-dotted Canadian plains of Ontario. Not until they reached the upper, many-fingered tributaries of the Garden River did they settle to feed and rest. Although the line bunched to a certain degree as they stopped, it was still strung out over several miles.

Surprisingly, it was warmer here than it had been in upper Michigan and the trees were more heavily budded. Hemlock and pine seeds abounded. Numerous tiny berries were already forming on low plants, and catkins on birch and alder thickets were numerous.

When he had eaten his fill, the young passenger pigeon rested for only a little while before he was ready to fly again, but the adults were content to doze in the warm sunlight as they digested their meal. The young bird bobbed his head a few times as if agitated and then shot upwards and winged toward the head of the flock. A half dozen of the younger birds rose from the ground to follow him, all but two of these settling back to the ground almost immediately.

The three birds — the young passenger pigeon, a male about his own size and a female considerably smaller — reached the leading edge of the grounded birds quickly and landed amongst them. Then, as placidly as if they had been there all the while, they nibbled contentedly on what food remained.

A rather peculiar thing was apparent now. While most of the adult passenger pigeons were of approximately the same size (with the males generally somewhat larger than the females), here at the forefront of the flock it was obvious that the birds were, on the whole, a bit larger than average. This was most apparent in comparison with the young female who had flown to the van with them. Far back in the flock she was smaller than most of the adult females, but not a great deal smaller. Here, however, there was a decided difference in size. Even the two young males, large as they were, were definitely smaller than these adults, though they had been more than a match in size for many of the adult males toward the rear.

Leadership of this flock was obviously not relegated to any one bird. At least two dozen huge males, resplendent in blue-gray and russet, were undoubtedly leaders among them, as were a third that many large females. Some of these birds were rather the worse for wear. Many had pinion feathers missing, and parts of their tails were gone. One male hopped about quite skillfully on one leg and two others were as alike as twins, right down to each of them missing his left eye.

The bird which stood out most to the young passenger pigeon, however, was a magnificent male who was larger than any other pigeon in sight. His eyes were large and very alert, constantly scanning both sky and ground around them for possible peril. But the factor which most set him apart from the others was a very pronounced melanism of his plumage. Instead of having head and back feathers of clear slate blue and a breast of red like the others, he was almost black all over.

His shoulders and head and back were a deep blue-black which somehow managed to retain that metallic bronze over the back of the neck. His breast was only a little lighter and was a rather rusty black. Instead of reddish pink, his feet were a deep gray, and even his eyes were a dark maroon instead of the scarlet of his fellows.

The other pigeons seemed to take this variance in color for granted, but the young passenger pigeon felt himself very drawn to the strangely colored male. He waddled close to him and watched as he picked up and swallowed a few seeds here, stopped and scratched his chin with his foot over there. When he dozed, the young bird sidled close to him and dozed as well and when he awakened, the young bird opened his eyes an instant later.

When the flock rose from the ground almost as one a little while later, the young passenger pigeon flew directly behind the big dark male and, though the air here was more difficult to fly through, he was content with his position so close to the leading line of birds.

Often during the following days there were segments of the flock which remained behind when they took off, and at least once or twice each day smaller groups of three or four hundred birds would angle away from the main body on their own.

Each time they stopped to feed or rest or take roost for the night, the young passenger pigeon remained relatively close to the dark bird. The melanistic pigeon paused and contemplated this stripling occasionally but he evinced no objection to being shadowed in this manner. One time, in fact, when he caught the young bird staring at him he puffed up his breast, leaned his head far back and strutted pompously a few steps before fluffing his feathers and returning to his feeding as if nothing had happened.

On the morning when this flock spread their wings to leave the sprawling "h" shape of Lake Missinaibi, nearly half of the flock elected to remain behind, including most of the young birds that had joined the flock with the juvenile passenger pigeon. This was of little concern to the young bird, however, and he continued his flight behind the dark bird he found so admirable.

The number of lakes in this rolling country was fantastic and at each of them there were huge armadas of swimming ducks and geese. Mallards quacked sonorously at them as they flew past and great rafts of Canada geese honked with a strangely stirring cry. Now and again a flock of canvasback ducks or teal would bullet past them in loose formation, and as they followed the Fire River north toward its junction with the Missinaibi they encountered a cloud of hundreds of thousands of dainty golden plovers, somewhat smaller than the passenger pigeons and so remarkably regimented that on a single wingbeat the entire flock would flare or dip or climb. This flock quickly disappeared toward its breeding ground in the Arctic Circle, but even after it had gone from sight the young passenger pigeon remained excited and deeply moved by its high-pitched and rapidly repeated flight cry of "*Coodle-coodle-coodle.*"

The Missinaibi River ran wide and swift, its deep waters a pleasing blue-green against the dun and olive of the turf bordering it. As they followed its great curve from almost due north until it was flowing directly eastward, the land became flatter, considerably more marshy and even more heavily populated with waterfowl. But it was not until they reached the salt-filled atmosphere in the tidal flats below the conjunctions of those four great Canadian rivers — the Missinaibi, the Moose, the Abitibi and the French — just before they dumped into the huge inland sea of James Bay, that southern bulge of Hudson Bay, that the flock settled down and then scattered.

Here, where on rare occasions the alien forms of caribou and occasional musk ox lumbered along on the higher ground in the distance, where dark otters sported at the water's edge and the great flights of snow geese and magnificent trumpeter swans split the clear blue sky with their sharp wedge formations; here where their dread enemy, man, was virtually non-existent; here was where the young passenger pigeon spent his first summer.

5

THE young passenger pigeon awoke with the eerie, piercing cry still echoing in his ears, and it stirred a restlessness in him. With half a hundred other pigeons he had been roosting in the lower branches of a thick balsam fir a quarter mile from the river, but now as the sound came again he flitted from branch to branch until he was at the top of the fifty-foot tree.

For the third time the weird laughing cry vibrated clearly through the morning air, and now the young passenger pigeon found its source. A large sharp-beaked bird raised itself high on the surface of the water and beat its wings with a faint drumming. Its back was glossy black with neat white checkerings and its breast, clearly visible as it flapped in this manner, was a startling white, as brilliant and unmarred as the willow-leaf patch of white on the young bird's own right wing.

He had not before seen such a bird nor heard the gripping, lonesome cry which is trademark of the loon, but with the sound of it the restlessness blooming within him increased to unusual proportions. He bobbed his own head nervously and a barely audible clucking escaped his bill.

With a final melancholy chattering scream, the loon began

skittering across the surface of the water. It appeared to be having difficulty rising, and the short stubby wings, definitely far too small for such a large-bodied bird, worked furiously to lift him.

The loon's speed increased, and though its body left the water its legs still pumped vigorously, and the wide webbed feet actually ran along the surface making rapid splattering sounds clearly audible to the bird in the balsam fir. And then, suddenly airborne, with its landing gear retracted, the yard-long bird sped away to the east at great speed and disappeared over the gray-green expanse of the foot of James Bay.

The young passenger pigeon, still wearing the drab brown of juvenile plumage, had grown larger and even more stream-lined during the summer. He had fed well on the extensive flats of cranberries, and his breast plumage had frequently been stained with the juice of blueberries. He had tasted and delighted in a wide variety of foods, both animal and vegetable, and while there were many things of which he was very fond, such as the tasty and plentiful pigeonberries, he searched in vain wherever he happened to be for the food that he liked best — beechnuts.

During this summer he had regained much of the weight lost in those first treacherous days out of the nest and all of the passengers were, after this pleasant interval of feeding and casual exploration, sleek and heavy.

The dark bird had been — and still was — a decidedly influencing factor in the juvenile passenger pigeon's education. All through their association during the summer the younger bird had observed him closely and, in many respects, emulated his actions perfectly. And though he certainly could not have been aware of it, he was learning from the dark bird a pattern of life that would protect him for as long as he lived.

During the early part of the summer he had been prone to remain in the thickest part of the congenial clusters of pigeons, but at such times the dark bird would disappear and almost always he would later be found on the very fringe of the flock, searching the surrounding countryside with his keen eye as much as joining the activities of the other birds.

More often than not the dark bird took off at great speed, leaping from the ground as if it had erupted beneath him and wheeling through the air in a dizzying series of maneuvers until he reached cruising altitude. For the young bird it was something of a game to follow closely on his tail, and little by little he became so adept at the maneuvers that only with the most concerted effort was the older bird able to shake him.

It soon had become second nature to the young passenger pigeon, continuing in this pattern established for him by the dark leader, to fly on the fringe of any flock with which he flew and seldom in the same position for very long. Sometimes it would be in the van, leading the big flock to new places for food and exploration. Just as often, however, he was content to follow the crowd, flying always at the edge, whether it was on the sides or tail end of the flight.

Time and again the two birds had gone off on their own, far from any of the other pigeons, but while it was great sport to move about like this for a little while, invariably a powerful desire too strong to resist would pull them back to the company of massed birds. It was not their nature to be solitary and when apart from others of their kind they quickly grew lonely.

From the dark pigeon he had learned other things as well. No longer did he select a landing spot from on high and fly directly down to it. Even when there were other pigeons down below murmuring over some deposit of food they had discovered, the pair would circle twice, three times, sometimes four or five times before abruptly plummeting earthward.

When alighting on isolated trees they would approach only a foot or so above the ground until nearly to the trunk, there to arrow upwards and spread out to land on the branches, holding their momentum until the last moment, when they braked with wildly beating wings and tail spread in a great fan.

On leaving such a tree they would plunge downward as if on a toboggan slide, and at high speed close to the ground they would skim off through avenues in the woods, only gradually rising above the trees.

The young passenger pigeon delighted most in following the dark bird at breakneck speed through a dense woods, flitting, angling, veering, dropping, flaring to avoid striking branches. Often a whole flock of several hundred would join them in this game, hurtling into a woods at full tilt and emerging from the other side without a single bird having touched branch or twig, maneuvering with an ability that was uncanny.

It was a happy, wonderful, carefree summer and he grew to love this wildly beautiful Ontario countryside. But where for over four months he had been content, the cry of the loon had unlocked an unease in his breast, and this same sensation seemed to be affecting the others.

The early October breeze rippled the blades of marsh grasses — grasses they had watched change from brilliant emerald to dull washed olive and then to a uniform tan as the nights grew colder and the days shortened — and this breeze brought from the north a promise of bitter weather and biting wind and endless snow.

Unlike the hundreds of other species of birds which summered this far north and spent many days in restless dartings and gatherings prior to migration, the passenger pigeons reached their decision to migrate and acted upon it at one and the same time. Where the sky had been virtually devoid of life only a moment ago, now it became filled with pigeons rising everywhere. They flung themselves up in singles and pairs, in tiny squads of eight or ten, in companies of a hundred or more and in thundering divisions of thousands.

For the first few minutes their flight was utterly confusing to all but themselves. Some flew east and others west. A few darted northward and still others angled to the south. Slowly they turned, all of them; turned and circled and returned, and the semblance of a formation developed. Twice, thrice, four times they winged their way around a circle with a diameter of more than a mile, and by the time the fourth transit had been completed there flew a monstrous halo of pigeons three hundred feet high over the river, and only scattered bands of pigeons still hustled to join the pattern.

The circle broke at its southeastern edge and unwound gracefully into a long stream of fifty thousand birds. They maintained their relatively low altitude and flew strongly in a line just a little south of due east. Within minutes they crossed the south rim of James Bay, winged over open water for some forty minutes and then arrowed back over land at the east foot of the bay. Ten minutes later they were in the Province of Quebec.

Scarcely a mile passed, as they continually angled more to a due south heading, when additional flights of passenger pigeons were not joining them, and later in the afternoon when they crossed the wide St. Lawrence River at Charlemagne, just fifteen miles seaward from Montreal, the flock was already a dozen miles long and a quarter mile wide.

Not until they had been skimming low over the waters of Lake Champlain for some time and darkness was rapidly approaching did they cross into New York State and alight to feed and roost in the heavily wooded hills of the Adirondacks. And when at dawn the flock aroused, a contingent of perhaps six hundred birds had already been gone for an hour, seeking out a mid-morning feeding place for the flock.

The principal body of birds took wing again while the woods were still hazy with the gloom of early light, but rising swiftly they burst into sunlight. Scarcely five miles were traversed when another flock fully as large as their own angled toward them low over the water from the northeast, from over the Green Mountains of Vermont. The higher flock dipped, and the two bodies of birds met and merged only thirty feet above the waters of the lake. As they jockeyed for position, the column stretched even farther back.

The young passenger pigeon had been in the midpoint of the circling halo of birds when it broke and left James Bay, and little by little he had moved forward in the flock, studying the birds around him carefully, seeking one in particular. He didn't find him. In fact, it wasn't until they had been airborne for two hours this second morning that he saw the familiar shape of the large, dark leader several birds behind the leading edge of the flock and far on the western rim.

Between the two during the summer had grown a peculiar sort of bond, a happiness at being close together and a sensation approaching that of distress at being apart. Few were the days when they hadn't flown together for at least a little while.

But when the flock assembled they had been roosting miles apart and the dark bird, instead of being near the lead, brought up the rear, apparently content to remain there for the first day's flight. After the night's rest he had been one of the six hundred who left to precede the main body an hour before dawn, but then he had curiously changed his mind and angled back down to the trees as the smaller flock flew south.

When the dawn flight of the main column had begun, he had been more than a mile to the southwest of it, but he was in the air quickly when he heard them rise and a burst of speed which whipped him along at better than eighty miles per hour soon permitted him to intercept and join the leading edge of the flock. It was here that the young bird found him.

Although the youngster made no vocal sound when he fell

into place beside the dark bird, matching his wingbeats exactly, he was aware that the older bird knew he was there and there was a sense of comfort in this, a deep warm pleasure that they were flying together once more.

The manner in which small flights of passenger pigeons had joined the flock yesterday as it sailed over the wilderness of Quebec prairies had been impressive, but it was as nothing compared to the number which constantly joined the flock now. From every quarter they came, a continuing procession of birds winging toward them as if the main flock were a great whirlwind and the individual scattered birds and small flocks were motes of dust being sucked into the vortex. In two hours the flock had redoubled its size and, though still considerably smaller than that flock which had winged its way north from the Gulf Coast the preceding spring, it was nevertheless of impressive size. They flew six or seven birds deep on a front of a half mile, and from end to end the column was forty-two miles long.

They followed the Hudson River downstream for more than three hours and then, just above Poughkeepsie, were intercepted by a fifty-bird contingent from the scouts. These birds wheeled about and took position several hundred yards ahead of the main body and began leading the column in a wide curve to the west, crossing the high-hilled northern corner of New Jersey and sailing over Milford, Pennsylvania. Here, across the mighty Delaware River from the Kittatinny mountain range the scouts dipped sharply earthward and then joined the hundreds of birds which arose from the forest before them and sped away to the south.

The leaves were ablaze with color, splashed with orange and gold, brown, green, rust and scarlet as far as the eye could see and, more important, there had been a bounteous crop of mast: beechnuts and acorns, hickory and chestnuts, hazelnuts, mockernuts, butternuts and many more. The elms and maples were especially well seeded and the slopes of these forests were teeming with heavily berried shrubs — pokeweed and hackberry, elderberry and moonseed, cohosh, barberry, haw and sumac, holly, bittersweet and dozens of others.

They flew for another hour until the trailing end of the flight was just passing the area upon which the scouts had fed before they settled to feed for themselves. Because the naked branches of dead trees were easier to light upon, great numbers of birds headed for them and piled one atop another until the roar of wings was punctuated by the fearful snapping of branches and toppling of entire skeletal trees.

The ground became an incredibly dense blanket of fluttering birds feeding voraciously. And when, an hour later, fed and rested, the now perching flock took wing and headed south again, many hundreds of dead and injured birds were left behind. This was as it had always been and it remained of no concern to the survivors. Only those being abandoned cried out in anguish and fear, and for the majority of them the end was close. A multitude of forest predators were well aware that the great pigeon flock had landed to feed here and already they were converging toward the area where they knew there would be injured and dead birds aplenty left behind in the denuded area.

Over level ground the flock normally flew at a height of

five hundred feet or higher, but in hilly or mountainous country, such as this, they tended to follow valleys and sweep along close to the treetops. Time after time gunfire would come from below and each time, depending upon the flock's altitude, birds would drop — two or three or possibly even a half dozen if the flock was high, but scores and even a hundred or more of them at each shot if the birds were flying low enough for effective scatter-gunning.

At each burst of gunfire the section of the column approaching this point would veer and swing wide and the remainder of the flock would follow this maneuver. And since the gunfire was an almost constant thing, the extensive and constantly growing column of birds writhed through the sky like some fantastic serpent slithering through the hills.

Despite the hazards of repeatedly being shot at and attacked by birds of prey along the way, the young passenger pigeon exulted in this process of migration. The thunder of beating wings, the rush of air, the matching of wingbeat for wingbeat with neighboring pigeons, all these were a tonic to him, and as his strong wings carried him along effortlessly at a mile a minute he scanned with great interest the terrain over which they flew.

Less than an hour and a half after their mid-morning feeding they crossed the Susquehanna River a score of miles downstream from Harrisburg, and an hour later the flock curved gracefully around the northern outskirts of Frederick, Maryland.

Ever more birds were joining them, and when at last the

flock settled for the night in a noisy half-mile-wide band, the leading edge was twenty-five miles south of Richmond, Virginia, on the banks of the Appomattox, and the line of birds clustered on every branch of every tree to the north all the way to the Rappahannock, one hundred miles behind.

It was an unfortunate place to stop, for the head of the column was only a dozen miles from Petersburg, its body only five miles west of Richmond, and its tail end actually in the outskirts of Fredericksburg. And just as the flock had attracted other passenger pigeons during the day, so now while it rested at night it attracted its most deadly enemy.

Only now and again during the night did the clanking of nearby railroad cars and wagons and the occasional sound of voices come to the young passenger over the prevailing din of fluttering wings and breaking branches and calling birds, but it was enough to make him and the birds about him nervous, and sleep was a fitful thing. A faint memory of the murmur of other wagons and voices at another time rose to haunt the young bird and even during those rare times when his eyes did close and he slept, occasional tremblings would set his plumage aquiver.

It was not a falsely founded fear. Word of the roosting column had spread swiftly by telegraph and word of mouth, and dozens, hundreds, thousands of men and boys in the three distant cities and in the area in between them hustled to the column in trains and wagons, on horseback and afoot.

By three o'clock in the morning the invaders had slipped into the woods, and while the gunners positioned themselves among the densest concentrations of birds to await daylight, the boys armed with sticks and gunny sacks roamed through the woods and in the dim moonlight clubbed to death every roosting pigeon within reach on the lower branches.

The higher birds were frightened by the sounds from below and yet, not themselves threatened, they remained in their trees and slept a restless sleep, weary after their long day's flight.

The greatest number of men had spread out among the birds in the vicinities of Richmond and Fredericksburg, but well over three hundred of them infiltrated the head of the column near Petersburg where the young passenger pigeon roosted beside the dark bird. The latter was far more nervous than he, bobbing his head and fluttering his wings most of the night. A soft clicking sound, echoed by dozens of other birds within hearing, came from his throat ceaselessly.

The wisdom of the dark leader's desire to stay on the fringe of the flock was evident now, for these two birds were very fortunate in their position. Even with other pigeons constantly joining the flock during the day, they had managed to keep at the very southwest edge of the column. When the men from Petersburg aligned themselves at intervals around the front of the column and then slowly entered the woods, they did not stop until they were many yards in and past the two birds. And even though the young passenger pigeon and the dark leader could hear the muted sounds of clubs striking those birds perched closer to the ground, they could see nothing of the danger and so they remained where they were, nervous but not overly alarmed.

An hour before dawn there came to these two the distant sound of gunfire, but it quickly faded and shortly thereafter in the darkness above them they heard the wingbeats of the large scouting party as it headed southward. The noise of the youngsters swinging their clubs below had long since ceased, and in that interval of deep darkness between moonset and dawn the forest became deceptively quiet. It seemed almost peaceful here as from a distance came the faint crowing of a rooster at a farmhouse.

That this was merely an illusion became dreadfully apparent as the light of dawn threw the bird-laden trees into sharp silhouette against the sky. One moment there was no sound, and in the next instant a gun was fired and instantly followed by a tremendous barrage of shooting sweeping the entire column. One old pigeon hunter pointed his ten-gauge shotgun loaded with fine shot at an angle and fired once, and with this single shot brought down dead or injured a total of one hundred eighty-seven birds.

At the first shootings the flock left their perches and beat their way into the sky, but the carnage grew even worse. Farther away from the guns now, the shot patterns from these weapons spread wider and killed even more. The bodies of pigeons thumped to the ground in a steady hail.

Sticking to their long-established pattern of flying low over the trees, the dense funnel of birds thundered south. For close to two hours the Petersburg hunters fired into the column as fast as they could reload, and at each shot from these men another dozen, another score, another hundred birds perished. And when at last the flock left the winding Appomattox behind, the men lay down their guns and bent to the task of putting into their sacks as many as they could carry of the over one hundred thousand birds they had slain.

They were quite selective about the birds they took, these hunters, preferring those not badly damaged. Birds with wings or breasts or abdomens all but shot away were tossed aside, as were the smaller birds. Only the biggest, fattest, heaviest-breasted birds were wanted. Later in the day, after the hunters and their offspring had departed, the nearby farmers drove their hogs to the woods and turned them loose to feed upon the tens of thousands of carcasses left lying.

This was the last day of the southward migration for the flock and for many of the birds flying therein it was the last day of life as well. For as the birds thrust their way south away from this scene of tragedy, birds by the hundreds continued to be left behind all the way. These were the wounded. Some flew only a mile or so before collapsing and tumbling crazily to the forest below. Others gradually lost altitude, found themselves unable to keep up and landed. Some of these latter birds would survive, but for the majority of them it was only a matter of time until they died of hunger or thirst or infection or were torn apart by predators. The cougars and bears, the scattered wolves, the foxes and owls and hawks in this wilderness dined well for many days.

There was no stop made this morning for feeding, and even after the column had flown across the tangled Green Swamp of North Carolina and thundered into a sharp column right when they hit the Atlantic coastline a dozen miles west of Cape Fear in mid-morning, they continued flying.

This first sight of the trackless expanse of ocean thrilled and startled the young bird. He had seen many lakes, of course, and had even flown across the foot of James Bay and down the entire length of long Lake Champlain, but they were as nothing compared to this water that stretched onward beyond his vision, seemingly to infinity. The great barren sand beaches below looked inviting and yet, though the flock lowered until it was flying no more than thirty feet above the water's edge, they did not land.

In half an hour the flock had crossed into South Carolina and continued winging along above the sands of Myrtle Beach. It was here that a contingent of scouts intercepted them and flew ahead of the main body, but when they turned inland toward the confluence of the Pee Dee and Waccamaw Rivers, the flock continued along the coastline and the scouts reluctantly fell in behind.

The smell of the salt in the air was affecting the young bird and many like him in a strange way. An odd chatter rolled from his beak, and often he dipped sharply in a dive, recovering with such precision that his breast feathers barely brushed the warm sand. Other birds began doing the same thing and it gave the impression of balls falling out of the low flying mass, hitting the ground and bouncing right back into the flock.

Where the coastline broke into little bays and inlets and islands the birds flew directly over the deep blue water and at such times dropped down to within inches of the highest swells. No less than a dozen times between Myrtle Beach and the Florida border they were fired upon by individual gunners

lying in wait for migrating waterfowl. No attempt was made
to pick up the pigeons that were thus downed, their sole
function having been one of providing targets.

Despite those shootings and occasional attacks by hawks,
however, the flock reached the mouth of the St. Johns River
at three o'clock in the afternoon. Flying low over the dark
water they left the ocean and followed the river's course upstream. The startled residents of Jacksonville rushed outside
to see this phenomenon of a dark river of birds streaming
along above the dark river of water, and while the first third
of the column passed by the city unscathed, the last two-
thirds came under a continuous gunfire. By the time the flock
was past, the surface of the river was gray and brown with the
bobbing bodies of many hundreds of pigeons being swept out
to sea.

It was a markedly different type of countryside down below now, unlike any the young passenger pigeon had seen
before. Strange slick-leaved oaks were bedecked with streamers of Spanish moss, and forests of spindly pines intermingled
with great patches of bare sandy land and vast stretches of
palmetto with foliage like pineapples, and there were also
undulating seas of lush grasses.

A huge segment of the flock to the left of the pair disengaged
itself and flew off to the east and another group of well over
a thousand birds directly behind them spiraled to the ground
below, looking for all the world like the funnel of a tornado
dipping down from a storm cloud.

The breaking up of the flock became more pronounced
every mile, and by the time the young bird and his companion

reached the expanse of Lake George, less than ten thousand birds were still flying with them.

A moment later the dark bird flared off at an angle to the west and the young passenger pigeon and two score other birds, both young and old, were with him on the next wingbeat.

The older bird appeared to be looking for something, and after another twenty minutes he abruptly flared again and then began to circle a bubbling spring below. The little flock followed and they alighted on the salt-encrusted rim of the spring.

The passenger pigeons had reached their winter home.

6

I T was an idyllic winter in Florida for the young passenger pigeon. For the most part the weather was quite warm, even on the frequent cloudy days. Except for the areas near the widely scattered cities and villages, there were remarkably few people.

Hazards were there, naturally, for the passenger pigeon had many enemies. There were hawks and eagles all too eager to snatch the careless bird, as well as mink and raccoons, bobcats and other predators, all having a taste for pigeon meat. But persecution from the most dangerous and most implacable enemy — man — was encountered only rarely and never in mass onslaughts as in the north.

Florida was a land of wondrous sights and a haven for more species of birds than the young pigeon knew existed. The air was constantly alive with the songs of this multitude; larks and bluebirds, finches and plovers, doves and cuckoos and flycatchers, kingfishers and warblers and hummingbirds.

Every creek, every pond, every lake was alive with ducks and herons, snipe and stilts and sandpipers. Stately sandhill cranes towered on sandbars and immaculate white egrets — some with legs of bright yellow, others with entirely black legs and still others with the entire shank of the leg black and just the foot encased in a brilliant yellow glove — perched on low branches over watercourses or stood quietly on their girder legs in the shallows as they waited patiently for imprudent fish and frogs.

Jays screamed raucously here and there in the pines, while red-winged blackbirds and yellow-headed blackbirds and bobolinks appeared and disappeared in tall reeds and grasses and sometimes perched and bobbed up and down precariously on long, slender stems.

Even though the en masse migration had ended for the passenger pigeons, there was still a gradual movement to the south. In no hurry to get anywhere now, the young bird and dark male, along with twenty others from their flock, meandered casually day after day down the center of this great peninsula. Accustomed to seeing lakes in great numbers in Michigan and Canada but relatively few during the southern migration, it was a delight to the young bird to discover virtually thousands of lakes in this country. And each of these lakes, each of the ponds and pools and great bubbling springs had its complement of wildlife beyond anything the young bird had ever before witnessed.

There were more hawks here, too, than he'd ever seen except for his first day out of the nest, but the fear they inspired was soon eased when it became obvious that they were far more interested in quarry easier to catch than agile pigeons. Mice and muskrats, voles and rabbits, frogs and crayfish and insects were abundant and made up the majority of their diets.

The little flock of pigeons stopped for several weeks at the northern end of huge Lake Okeechobee, and the abundance of food was staggering. Berries and succulents of all kinds, seeds of infinite variety, plump crickets and grasshoppers were everywhere. Salt springs were numerous, and the pigeons spent many hours nibbling the white crystals and picking up grit at the various deposits.

At the end of the third week there, after roosting all night in a thicket of stunted live oaks less than eight feet high, the young passenger pigeon awakened to see his dark companion already on the ground nearby drinking from a little pool. Several of the other birds opened their eyes and watched sleepily as he joined the dark bird, but they made no attempt to follow. When the two birds leaped into the air and sped southward, the others elected to stay behind and so now, for the first time since their flights together in Ontario, the young passenger pigeon and his older companion were alone.

They continued their southward meandering, sporadically joining with small groups of passengers for a day or so, but eventually moving on by themselves. For three days as they moved even farther south beyond their normal range they were accompanied by a group of five other passengers, one of whom was a huge female of unreasonably aggressive nature. Although the courting season was months away, for some reason she seemed to take a shine to the dark male, while at the same time displaying a high degree of belligerancy toward the young passenger pigeon. She followed the dark male's every move, and twice bowled the young bird over when he came too close to them.

This harassment might have resulted in the young bird's eventually flying off on his own had it continued, but fate took a hand. As the little flock alighted in a mangrove tangle at the edge of a high hammock in the sprawling Everglades, the dark male continued to the ground a foot or so from the water's edge. He waddled to the shoreline and began to drink, and immediately the big female fluttered downward from her perch. Instead of landing on shore, however, she alighted on one of a pair of half sunken logs near shore, and as she dipped her head to the water the other log came to lightning-quick life.

The female's reflexes were good but not good enough. She leaped upward, but the small alligator neatly snapped her out of the air. He was only four feet long but the powerful jaws crushed her instantly, and just that swiftly he was gone with her in a thrashing swirl of the brown waters.

Even as the attack took place the dark male shot away in that peculiar zigzagging flight pattern, the young male close behind. The other four birds took to the air, too, but quickly settled to the mangroves again, confused over the disappearance of their leader.

Before long the pair found themselves over an area of thousands of mangrove islands, beyond which was the open sea. Some of these islands had narrow sandy beaches but mostly they were merely clusters of interwoven mangrove trees with their roots sheathed in a bristling armor of barnacles. These gray-barked trees grew from low islands thirty or forty feet in diameter comprised mostly of oyster shell on a pitted coral base.

This was the region known as the Ten Thousand Islands area, and it was a fascinating and somewhat frightening place for the pigeons to be and one only very rarely visited by the passengers. And while the two did not long remain here, they saw a great many unusual sights as they moved slowly northwestward from island to island.

The water was slightly murky, carrying suspended in it the traces of mud and decay from the thousands of rivulets emptying into the sea from the Everglades. It was generally shallow water and quite often vast banks of oysters or badly pitted and eroded coral upthrustings were exposed at low tides and formed gathering places for a wide variety of terns and gulls, pelicans and herons and spoonbills. On these newly exposed sections of real estate they either sat and dozed complacently or searched diligently for the delicacies of the sea which seemed to thrive in every coral crevice, in each discarded shell and in any other place that might provide some modicum of protection.

Often these sea and shore birds fed upon tiny fish marooned by the outgoing tide, and on the edge of the water, regardless of the tide stage, they could always find an abundance — an incredible abundance — of life. Fiddler crabs by the uncountable billions lined the shores and waved their ludicrous oversized claws at one another. Weird armor-plated chitons clung quietly to roots or rocks awaiting the return of the tide to resume their feeding. Snapping shrimp clicked and rattled menacingly in their tiny coral caverns, and shy hermit crabs lumbered along awkwardly, carrying on their backs the huge empty conch shells they had adopted as homes and fortresses.

Here and there the starfish that had been feeding upon coon oysters were exposed by the receding waters and slowly slid back into the protective liquid of the sea. The tangled roots of the mangroves projecting from the water were alive with sea roaches darting about swiftly in constant terror of a multitude of feathered and finned enemies. Higher in the branches were beautifully checkered and striped snails, and in the shallow-water areas where sea grass writhed in the currents, the tiny green shrimp and sea horses dared to come near the surface, while brick-red horse conchs methodically sought mollusks to devour.

Along the drop-offs and in the channels that wove around the islands were larger and more fearsome creatures. Solitary barracudas and sharks prowled in search of prey. Huge silvery tarpon six feet or more in length lazed just beneath the surface or broke water in arching rolls. Large vicious snook lay camouflaged beneath submerged mangrove roots, ready to flash out in an instant to snatch unwary passing shrimp or fish. Slender, bright green needlefish skittered along the surface, and occasionally fierce mangrove snappers splashed the surface as they captured some luckless fallen insect.

The piercing exhalation of air from porpoises breaking the surface was not uncommon and once, only a dozen yards from where the two passenger pigeons perched on a tiny key, a leopard ray more than five feet across the wingtips shot out of the water in a spectacular leap, and the sound it made as it slapped back onto the surface was like the crash of a cannon and frightened them.

Another time, when they alighted on one of the outermost

of the islands with a definite sand beach to the seaward side, the water was considerably clearer. As they sat upon the uppermost branch of a scraggly, wind-whipped pine and watched a trio of raccoons meandering along the shoreline, they also spied a leviathan loggerhead turtle fully five feet across the shell surge into the shallow water. It nosed about for a little while and then found and picked up from the bottom a large black conch. With unrelenting pressure its jaws clamped down on the hard shell until suddenly it shattered, and the exposed half-pound of conch meat was greedily devoured.

The larger islands, particularly those where the ground became more firm and was separated from the land mass of the Everglades proper only by narrow channels of fresh water running to the sea, were inhabited by a variety of wildlife. Water snakes and moccasins were abundant, as were alligators, and often the booming bellow of the latter could be heard distinctly.

Even farther north in the Glades, where the land became much more firm and the clustered mangroves began giving way to stands of towering bald cypress trees, there were herds of tiny deer and frequent prowling swamp bobcats. Raccoons were numerous beyond belief, and occasionally the pigeons spied cougars moving about stealthily from hammock to hammock, hunting the little deer they found so delectable.

In the great stands of cypress it seemed that practically every branch had its complement of yucca-like air plants and massed orchid bulbs and the air was redolent of moisture and the sweet, strangely stirring aroma of decay and newly sprouted plant life.

Farther to the north the birds wandered, and here the ground was quite firm and sandy, filled with palmetto and impressive stands of pine. On the shore of Lake Trafford near Immokalee they saw the first flock of passengers they had seen for many days and joined it with excited cries, and the reunion with their own kind was a wonderful experience.

There were thirty birds here, and together they dozed and waddled about and snuggled comfortably in the warm sand. The young passenger pigeon liked this area. There was an abundance of seeds and delicious insects, there was fresh water and there was good weather. Above all, there was the company of his own kind which he missed more than he had realized.

For more than a week they lingered, until late one afternoon when they had finished feeding at a nearby salt spring and were preparing to roost. All but the dark leader had settled down in preliminary napping on low palmetto branches around the spring, but he had become intrigued by the purposeful lumbering of a large brown beetle.

It moved rather rapidly, and despite the difference between their sizes the dark bird was hard put to keep pace with the insect. So intent was he upon doing so that he made the serious mistake of forgetting his surroundings. He waddled behind carelessly, occasionally nudging the beetle with his beak.

Twelve feet from the spring the beetle rounded a low palmetto growth and unhesitatingly the large dark bird followed it . . . and in that instant was struck and held in the jaws of a large Eastern diamondback rattlesnake.

The dark male shrieked in anguish and struggled fiercely but the rattler, fully six feet in length and several inches thick, writhed around the bird, pinning it to the ground, and the pigeon's exertions diminished.

At the big bird's initial cry of alarm the other passengers took off, then alighted immediately high in a nearby pine. In a moment they took to the air again, but the young bird remained on his perch. From here he watched in horror and fear the end of his companion.

After fully five minutes without motion, the snake released its bite, loosened its coils a little and took the dark bird's head in his mouth. Using its coiled body to help force the body farther in, the snake opened its mouth wider and wider, and waves of muscle action rippled down its length as the bird was ingested. In ten minutes only the sharp dark tail projected from the reptile's mouth, and then even that disappeared with one final convulsive swallow. The snake lay quiet and relaxed with its long forked tongue flicking in and out, and then it slowly slithered off and out of sight in the palmetto scrub. Except for a rather elongated swelling a foot or so behind its head, there was no indication that the dark pigeon had ever existed.

The young passenger pigeon remained in the pine for nearly an hour. In the gathering dusk he finally fluttered cautiously down to the palmettos flanking the salt spring and called softly, but there was no answer. He flew back to the pine and, after another few minutes, repeated the action.

For three full minutes he perched silently atop the palmetto. A little gust of air murmured through the pines with mournful whisper, then dipped to the ground and lofted a single black feather into the air. It whirled gracefully in a little eddy of air and then drifted gently down and landed on the surface of the spring. The current caught it and carried it out of sight down a little wavering rivulet.

The young passenger pigeon trembled, and a low whining sound issued from his partially opened beak. Finally he took wing and this time he did not stop. Already a great loneliness was filling him and he wanted the company of his own kind.

7

AFTER an auspicious beginning, the northward migration that spring had become a journey of demoralizing misfortune. The waters of the great lake glinted coldly beneath him and a weariness beyond any he had ever experienced made itself known in every muscle and bone in the yearling passenger pigeon's body. Now, when the entire flock should have been stopping for desperately needed food and rest, they had no choice but to continue the flight across this wide expanse of Lake Michigan.

During the last two weeks in Florida he had mingled with the passenger pigeons gradually drawing together in the wild open country some miles to the east of Tampa Bay. When he had first arrived there with a flight of forty other birds, there were several hundred pigeons gathered, but with more coming in every day the waiting birds numbered well over a thousand when the migrating column hove into view from the southeast.

The yearling passenger pigeon was ready for it. He had, during the last weeks of winter, lost the last vestige of juvenile plumage and now, in early March, was a truly fine specimen. The initial chestnut coloration of his eyes had become the blazing scarlet of his father's and his head and shoulders and back were a rich slate blue. His breast was slightly redder than

most of the males' and his feet were a startling reddish pink.
The sharply tapered brown-gray tail was fringed with white
feathers which, when spread, formed a perfect fan with what
seemed to be a fine lace edging. The only trace remaining of
his former coloration was the pure white willow-leaf patch on
his wing.

The flock which came toward them in the early light was
not yet very large. From their perches in pines and palmettos,
the Tampa birds could see both beginning and end of it; an
oval shape some two miles long and scarcely more than a mile
in breadth.

Theirs, however, was not the only contingent to join this
flock, and by the time they had crossed into Georgia over the
swampy course of the Suwanee River their oval had become
a column, still as wide but fully eighteen miles long. In the
area of northern Florida and southern Georgia there was a
constant incidence of pigeon bands joining them, and at eleven
o'clock that morning, when the advance scouts led them to a
feeding area rich with food along the banks of the Ocmulgee
River just south of Macon, the flock was a half-mile wide and
stretched out behind the leaders for seventy miles.

The men of Macon and the surrounding area had seen the
scouting flock alight, watched them feed and seen the little
group head back south to meet and guide the main flock. Thus
it was that several hundred armed men were waiting for them
and wherever the oncoming pigeons swooped to the trees they
converged. Georgia had not resounded to such a fusillade
since Sherman's men had ravaged the countryside.

Not all of the birds came under immediate fire, of course,

and some of them even managed to fill their crops and rest a bit before the migration resumed. The yearling passenger pigeon, however, was not among that fortunate number.

On the leading edge of the flock, he landed with them in a stand of timber, and though he immediately began the branch-by-branch dropping to the forest floor he never reached it. A volley of shots rang out and birds all around him fell.

He shrieked an alarm and strove to get away, but the very numbers of the birds worked against him and the others. Those birds far back in the column and still coming in collided with those rising to escape, and as many birds fell dead or injured through striking one another as were shot. A single shotgun blast in this thickly bird-packed air never brought down fewer than fifty birds and more often well over a hundred.

The yearling broke free at last and shot high into the air, minus a few feathers and with one wing hurting badly from being hit by a plummeting pigeon. A semblance of organization was resuming, and while the carnage continued unabated below the leaders streaked away to the north, and those still able to fly trailed them in a helter-skelter line.

Having retaken his position on the leading rim of the column, the yearling passenger pigeon helped to set a rather faster than usual pace. The sharp pain in his wing had quickly diminished until it had become a steady bone-deep ache which annoyed him considerably but did not seriously affect his flight.

Having re-formed now with some thirty thousand fewer birds than had arrived at the feeding area, the column progressed northward at a steady sixty-five miles per hour, and by the end of an hour only an occasional bird dropped dead or was forced to spiral downward.

The altitude of the flock lowered to within one hundred feet of the ground and its speed decreased by ten miles an hour as they entered the mountainous country to the north of Atlanta. More pigeons continued to join them, and by the time the whole of Tennessee had been crossed and the Cumberland River wound through Kentucky's hills beneath them, the column was well over one hundred miles in length.

The northern slopes of the Appalachians held a bitter surprise, for instead of dark forests filled with acorns and beechnuts to make up for the food they had missed at the morning feeding, the birds found an area covered by more than a foot of heavy snow thickly crusted on top as the result of a hard freeze. There was still more than an hour of daylight remaining, and the flock continued flying at slightly increased altitude as the country leveled out. The speed of the column reduced even more as the leaders scanned the white ground far ahead for a spreading darkness which would indicate an end of the snow cover and food as well as rest.

The result of this slowing in front was that the flock spread and thickened into such a great cloud that it brought Kentuckians out into the frigid air to watch the awesome sight. And even as the birds began settling in a heavily wooded tract along the Salt River just south of Louisville at twilight, already the wires were humming with word of this flock and the hunters came.

It took time to assemble, for they came from Louisville and Frankfort and even from as far away as Lexington. The roosting area was too huge by far to attempt surrounding it, since it was eight miles wide at the front and shaped something like a huge teardrop with the tail tapering back all the way to Cumberland Falls, but by one o'clock in the morning some four thousand men were lined up. They planned their assault carefully, allowing a space of about ten feet between each other. At that they were hardly able to effectively cover the front edge of the roost.

A word-of-mouth signal ran down the line, and the men stepped into the woods and began their work of clubbing the birds roosting close to the ground. It was hard work and soon the men were perspiring and opened their heavy coats despite the cold.

The pigeons were well aware the men were there, but it was nighttime and they didn't like flying in darkness. Furthermore, their day's long flight without a mid-morning rest and without the food that they should have had had severely sapped them, and so those higher in the trees simply watched with a stupid fatalism as their lower brethren were slain by the tens of thousands.

Not until three hours had passed and some of the men forsook the club for guns and the explosions grew more and more frequent did the weary birds take wing again, even though the darkness remained.

Now all the guns came to life, and though the birds could

not be seen in the darkness above, the roar of their flight was deafening, and all the hunters had to do was load, raise and fire methodically until their ammunition was expended.

It was a dreadful slaughter and it didn't end there. Sporadically from the darkness below as the flock winged north over Louisville and across the Ohio River into Indiana, the blinking red of gunfire was encountered and birds continued to fall. Between Bardstown, Kentucky, and the Ohio River no less than two hundred thousand passenger pigeons lay dead or wounded upon the snow as the bleak gray light of morning streaked the eastern sky.

By that time the van of the flock was approaching Logansport, Indiana — tired and hungry with still no food available because of the snow and no resting place safe because of the continued harassment as they progressed, even though now they had climbed to five hundred feet and were out of shotgun range. Rifles still spoke here and there, and it was rare indeed when a single bullet did not bring down two or more birds.

By eight o'clock the front of the flock had crossed into Michigan and encountered the great lake at Benton Harbor. And here, where they might well have expected snow, the ground was clear and the possibility of finding a place to feed and rest was greatly improved.

But now it was nature's hand which turned against them, for last fall had been a very poor one for the mast crop here, and there was little available to eat. What few beechnuts and acorns had matured and fallen the preceding autumn had long since been devoured by jays and grouse and the multitude of birds and mammals that wintered in this area.

In the rolling expanse of woods that stretched out to the north and east and south from the mouth of the Kalamazoo River they stopped and clustered dejectedly in trees and shrubs and on the ground, and though here and there an edible morsel was found, the birds remained hungry.

Their rest lasted less than an hour. Hunters had begun collecting along the eastern edge of the column, and though the toll they took was small, it was time to move away again before the siege increased. The day was warming considerably and the older adults of the flock led the birds north along the Lake Michigan shoreline.

This coast actually angled north-northwest for some time but then, at Little Sable Point, it first curved straight to the north and then began swinging to a northeast bearing. Without hesitation the old leaders turned sharply to the left and led the flock over the dark calm waters of the open lake, flying due west.

And so now, here they were, flapping across the lake and every one of them plagued with a weariness the like of which he had never known. The young passenger pigeon flew doggedly, his wings leaden and difficult to raise on the upbeat, too willing to collapse on the downbeat.

It was only a hundred and ten miles across the lake at this point to Sheboygan, Wisconsin, and even in their weary, hungry state, it was not a flight every one of them couldn't make normally. Twice during this flight from Florida the fist of nature had pounded them — first with the heavy snows north of the Appalachians and then with the lack of mast in southwest Michigan — and now came the third and most punishing blow.

As the birds approached the halfway point they entered a great cloud hanging low over the water. Too late the realization came that this was not just another cloud, for they did not quickly break through it to open daylight on the opposite side. This was one of the heavy and paralyzing spring fogs which frequently blanket the lake, and within minutes of entering it the birds' sense of direction was nullified.

The result was a panic which raced through the flock, causing the birds to break pace, wheel, rise, dip, turn and circle helplessly. There were frequent collisions and the sounds of pigeons hitting the water was like the sound of many horses cantering through hoof-deep puddles.

The yearling passenger pigeon was terrified and he climbed ever higher to get away from the fatal milling of his companions. It was a fear which grew because of his very helplessness, his inability to find direction and even a greater difficulty in maintaining balance. Always before in the face of danger he could flee and the danger was soon behind him, but now it was everywhere, constantly with him, dogging his every wingbeat and buffeting his head in a damp sticky way that made flying progressively harder.

A cluster of rising birds narrowly missed colliding with him and he joined them, able to see only the bird ahead of him with any degree of clarity, the bird ahead of that one just dimly, and beyond that, nothing.

The world had become a nightmare of beating wings, of

eyes straining to see against this outer blindness, of raw and persistent fear. Abruptly he missed a turning of the bird ahead, and though he made up for it an instant later, he had lost the little group. A minute later he heard the thrashing wings of another, larger group and he angled toward the sound and joined them.

A quarter-hour, half-hour, full hour passed and still they flew blindly. The moisture permeating the feathers made them all logy and flying an ever-increasing difficulty. He felt they were losing altitude but he couldn't be sure until suddenly a bird below splashed heavily into the water. Then others were hitting and once more he strained to rise from this new peril. Others climbed with him and they rose higher and higher yet until his lungs were twin fires in his breast and his heart a terrible hammer that threatened to pound its way free of the encircling flesh.

And then, as suddenly as they had entered the fog, they burst into clear air, and the blaze of the sun beating down was as welcome a sight as any of them had ever seen. Far, far ahead a thin, barely visible line indicated shore, and he winged toward it, leading the sixty or more birds that had broken out of the fog with him.

All around them other clusters of birds were coming out of the fog bank and slowly these clusters drew together and resumed flock formation, but they were thus far a pitiful remnant of the flock that had set off across this treacherous body of water.

In fifteen minutes they were over that desolate stretch of

shoreline between Sheboygan and Manitowac, and instantly they fluttered haphazardly to the ground, landing awkwardly on the sandy shore, plopping into tall dried grasses, clinging awkwardly, swayingly to the branches of stunted trees and bushes.

The yearling passenger pigeon had fluttered clumsily into a scrawny cedar tree and struggled to maintain his balance, eventually slumping to a crouch and leaning against the central body of the little tree. A few inches from him was a cluster of blue cedar berries, and by sidling along his perch a short way he was able to reach out and pluck them. When they were gone he looked for more, but the nearest cluster was more than a foot over his head and he just couldn't seem to bestir himself enough to go to them. He crouched again and slept.

From the area of fog far out over the lake a constant billowing of birds broke free as far as the eye could see in either direction and headed toward shore. Even the unskilled observer would have had no difficulty in detecting the unutterable weariness in flight of these passenger pigeons. Frequently there were those too weak or infirm to travel farther even though shore was now in sight and the still becalmed surface of the lake was punctuated with hundreds of thousands of tiny splashes as the birds fell, floundered and drowned.

Those that made it to this shore came in drunkenly, more often falling the last foot or two to the ground than actually executing a landing. These birds lay on the ground in such abject exhaustion that they were unable to move, not even when further birds came swooping in to tumble atop them. The sand of the shoreline became invisible under this mantle of birds two or three in depth endlessly up and down the coast.

Although the birds that survived this fog numbered still in the hundreds of millions, the loss of life to the flock was severe. Upon entering the fog the pigeons had spread in all directions, and only those fortunate enough to have continued flying in a basically easterly or westerly direction reached safety. Thus it was that almost half this tremendous flock of passenger pigeons perished in the frigid waters of the great lake.

The recuperative power of wild creatures is often little short of amazing, and it was apparent among these fatigued birds. Hardly more than an hour after plunging to the ground they began to show signs of awareness of their surroundings. Some of those not buried under a blanket of their fellows were able to stand on their own feet again and take some measure of interest in what they saw. All of them were ravenous, of course, but here and there they found seeds dropped from the sedge grass and other weeds and gobbled them quickly. A rather extensive cluster of hawthorn trees drew them like a magnet, and though the fruits that had fallen last autumn were old and the brilliant little red apples had long since become a wizened, rotted brown, they were nevertheless plentiful, and each contained large nourishing seeds, and so they were eaten avidly.

In this hour the yearling passenger pigeon had become much rested, though he was still weak and sore of muscle, and he fed heartily along with the others. Despite the large quantity of hawthorn apples that were on the ground they had vanished quickly, and now the birds began moving westward on the ground toward another maze of hawthorns in the distance. On the way they devoured every seed, every nut, every sprig of brave new growth.

It was at a point about midway through the second grove that the yearling found he could eat no more. His crop was heavy and tightly swelled and so he winged his way to a limb a dozen feet or more from the ground, perched there comfortably and was instantly asleep.

Even after the limbs around him and in the other trees of the grove were lined shoulder to shoulder with the pigeons, more kept coming. Some fluttered along from the direction of the lake, alternately touching the ground and then lofting raggedly a few feet before touching down again, but mostly they waddled in a queer feathered blanket and their sharp eyes sought out every speck of edible material along the way.

To both north and south the birds moved westward in an unbelievable mass. Those toward the rear still coming from the lake shore found little food and they continued walking toward the distant forest in a lemminglike flow.

This time the yearling passenger pigeon slept very soundly for three hours and awakened extremely refreshed, the stiffness of his muscles relaxed, the gnawing hunger gone and the desire to move upon him again. Already many of the birds were thrusting into the air to form a new column and he joined them without hesitation.

They flew to the west, and from the forest toward which the

weary birds had walked those hours ago fantastic clouds of pigeons rose to join them. Practically all of these birds flew with strong measured wingbeats, and it was a difficult thing to believe that only hours before they had undergone deathly hardship.

The sun was far in the west and they flew along its rays at a mile-gobbling pace. The respectable expanse of Lake Winnebago came into view ahead, then was under them, then behind them. They turned slightly to the north and in an hour more had skirted Stevens Point and followed the Wisconsin River upstream, flying low over the water past Rib Mountain and Wausau and Merrill.

With twilight fast closing on them, they angled away from the river toward the swampy wilds where food was plentiful and their greatest enemy scarce. And here, among the mixed pines and hardwoods in a spongy-earthed expanse to the west of the Wisconsin River and to the south of Tomahawk and to the east of Rib Lake, the great column of some nine hundred million passenger pigeons ended its northern migration.

8

SEVERAL days of desultory feeding and exploration in this Wisconsin River swampland satisfied the birds. It was an area of countless alder thickets, birches, scrub oaks and jack pines. Best of all, there had been a good mast crop here the preceding fall and the ground was quite liberally peppered with acorns. The catkins of the birches and alders and aspens were swelling, as were the buds of various shrubs and trees. It would be an excellent place to nest.

But now, having discovered such a place, the flock did a curious thing. Early in the morning of their third day here it rose and flew — not in a great column, but highly dispersed in squadrons and companies and divisions — scattering out of sight in every direction of the compass, as ripples move out from a pebble dropped into a pool.

The yearling passenger pigeon, well fed and well rested, found himself in the company of some forty thousand birds heading southwest. He flew lightly, strongly, the terror of the northward migration behind him and no longer a matter of concern. An uplifting effusion swept him and the others, and they dipped and swerved, rose and fell, zigzagged in stair-step fashion and put on bursts of speed that clove the air at ninety miles per hour.

Only when they had flown for over an hour and were winging along the Chippewa River south of Eau Claire did they circle a few times and then spiral down to a forest of oak to feed. As always when feeding in smaller groups like this, a corps of sentinels took their places in the branches of the tallest trees, ready to sound an alarm should danger threaten.

The feeding action engaged in here was a unique procedure. Having landed at the edge of the woods, they stretched out in a front that extended for fully a quarter of a mile, with a depth of about one hundred yards. All began feeding at the same time and there was a gradual movement into the woods. In a few moments, as might be expected, those in the rear found the ground stripped of mast and so they arose above the treetops and alighted directly in front of the advancing birds, who now stopped where they were. This process of rising from the rear and settling at the front became continuous and uniform and so smoothly executed that the whole flock presented the startling appearance of a great rolling cylinder with a diameter of about fifty yards and its interior filled with an incredible mixture of flying leaves and grasses and feathers. A hundred foundries could not have equaled the noise they made.

Left in peace this day, the birds took their time, fed well, rested all night and in the morning fed again. From this point on, their flights were short and apparently concerned only with food and rest. Yet, an unusual pattern was developing.

After flitting about and feeding well in an area for a day or two, they would fly many miles, passing by wonderful sources of food and other flocks of pigeons before settling down to repeat the process. There was a good reason for this. Soon it would become necessary to feed the squabs which would hatch, and they must know where food was available so as not to waste valuable time in fruitless searching.

Day by day the activity continued as they swung in a great arc counterclockwise. For some miles they followed the Mississippi River downstream as it flowed southeastward but when, at LaCrosse, the stream turned due south, they moved inland and once again came upon the Wisconsin River. This time they were in the Dell country where strange and fascinating rock formations pushed up from both the river and its shores like weird half-finished sculpturings by some giant carver.

Through these days and weeks of eating well, resting fully and casually exploring, a peculiar anticipation had been growing within the yearling passenger pigeon. Where always before it had been enough merely to be in company with the flock, that alone no longer sufficed. He found his attention taken more and more by the females of the flock, as if they had suddenly begun to glow. He watched them as they flew, delighting in their able maneuvering, impressed by their smooth lines and delicate beaks and feet. The alertness of their sparkling eyes, not scarlet like his but a hot orange-red, excited him, and when the flight of another male inadvertantly cut off his vision of one of these hens he became decidedly annoyed and often an irritable chattering cry would burst from him.

This period of relative ease and relaxation had been good

[113]

for them all. The reserves of fat so thoroughly used up in the perilous flight north were replenished. They filled out, even became a bit plump, and their colors had never been brighter or their plumage in better condition or their mood so happy and anticipatory.

They flew to the north now, paralleling the Wisconsin River ten miles to their west. And it was while they stopped at a great natural stone cluster projecting castle-like from swampy ground that the yearling passenger pigeon took special note of one particular female.

She was perhaps five years old and a beautiful hen. Though the bluish slate of her head and neck were certainly far duller than his own and the metallic luster of her shoulders and neck nowhere near as iridescent as his, still he found her the most attractive bird of the flock. She was smaller than he — no more than seventeen inches long — and though occasionally her glance settled upon him as he strove to keep close to her, there was a distinct reticence about her, a coquettishness which attracted him even further, rather than repelling him.

All the rest of the way north he stayed close to her and when, on the fourth day of April, they found themselves approaching the preselected nesting area the entire flock had abandoned close to a month before, his affection for her had become a deep need and desire.

From every direction the pigeons were returning and there was no hesitation in their flight, no indecision now about their destination. Never a moment passed during that day or the next or the one after that when the swarms of pigeons were not coming in to this central area. As they came there issued from them an unusual bell-like call, sweet and clear. With the thunder of their wings and the bell tones coming from these millions of birds at once, it gave the uncanny illusion of a great parade of horse-drawn sleighs approaching with bells tinkling merrily.

The yearling passenger pigeon's object of affection flew directly to a dense clump of scrub oaks stretching along the south bank of the Spirit River, and here she flashed through the branches in a remarkable display of maneuvering, her suitors hot upon her trail — for the yearling was by no means the only male that had been attracted by her demure beauty.

She landed on a branch fifteen feet high and at once the males engaged in a scrambling, rough-and-tumble, no-holds-barred battle on the ground beneath her. Two of these males were older than himself and all were smaller. With terrible thrashing of wings and stabbings of beaks — aimed always at the body and never at the eyes — they flew into one another, bowling each other over and striving to nip painfully at the tender skin beneath where the wings joined the body.

One by one they were vanquished. The largest of the older males was first to flee, a tuft of his feathers still clenched in the yearling's mouth. Brief skirmishes with two of the other birds — yearlings like himself — sent them fluttering away. The older male backed off a little and studied his youthful adversary. There was no denying the fire of fury burning in the young bird's eye or the strength which he possessed. At this point discretion became the better part of valor for the smaller bird. He hopped to a branch and then flashed to seek a less vied-for mate.

With immediate rivalry disposed of, the yearling turned his attention to the hen. He fluffed his feathers and flew to her perch, but as he landed she flew to the ground and he followed her there, a deep soft cooing issuing from him without pause. Initially she had displayed an aloof semi-interest in the scuffle between the males but now she became downright timorous. She flitted away and he followed. Ground to bush to tree to ground to tree they went, he never more than an inch or so behind, she never pausing more than an instant at each perch. Up and down, over and around they flew until finally she settled to the ground near that same spot where she had first alighted, and he thundered to the ground beside her.

The timidity disappeared from her demeanor and for the first time she showed an active interest in this aggressive and apparently dauntless young swain. The yearling, sensing this change, backed off several feet and shoved out his fiery breast. Farther and farther he puffed it out until at length his head was forced to rest on the feathers of his back and his bill pointed upwards. Standing like this he permitted his wings to droop until they touched the ground and then he fluffed his feathers to such an extent that every one of them seemed to be standing on end and he looked half again as large as normal. He spread his tail in an extraordinary wide fan and, with wingtips still dragging the ground, paraded back and forth in front of her, the ultimate in pomposity.

The hen bobbed her head a number of times as if quite

pleased with the display. At that the yearling returned to normal posture and leaped to the lowest branch of a nearby witch hazel shrub. His ridiculous feet gripped the branch with unsuspected strength and he raised his wings slowly until they were all but touching over his back. For thirty seconds he held this position and then he brought the wings down sharply. There was a crisp snapping sound as they struck the branch upon which he perched and then another sharper and louder sound similar to a whip cracking as he raised them swiftly until the pinion feathers slapped together over his back. Faster and faster this movement progressed until the white spot on his wing was a blur and the air resounded as if a string of firecrackers were going off.

The fact that literally millions of male birds were engaged in this same noisy practice at one and the same time created an inconceivable din. Had a bomb exploded in the center of this nesting area it probably would not have been heard at the outer edge.

A bit winded from this strenuous exercise, the yearling stopped. Briefly then, but with considerable showiness, he preened himself. As he was doing so the female flew to the uppermost branches of a twenty-foot scrub oak and at once two other males, both of them yearlings, flew to her side.

Instantly the young passenger pigeon flung himself to the attack. So savage was his fury that in only a few seconds the pair of interlopers were seeking less hazardous companionship.

The yearling returned to land on the same branch a foot from the hen and she eyed him intently with her head cocked slightly as he resumed his deep cooing. He sidled toward her and she did not retreat, and when he reached her side he pressed his body close to hers. With a final attempt at coyness, she sidled away a few inches and stopped. Undiscouraged, he repeated the move. This time she allowed him to stay close and from her own mouth came a little note of encouragement.

Standing high on the limb, the yearling passenger pigeon stretched his neck out and laid it across the back of the female's neck. He flexed his muscles and, using his beak as a sort of hook, pulled her head around toward him. She did not resist and when he released her she remained in this position.

Now he stooped and nudged her beak with his own until she opened it and he shoved his bill deep into her mouth, pulled free and then did it again. For long minutes after that their little bills rubbed gently together and every now and then the female would softly grip his bill in hers or he would take hers in his. This billing and cooing left no doubt that they had found one another entirely acceptable as mates.

This was the time to culminate the great need that nature had instilled in them both. With unexpected suddenness the female dropped to the ground and he followed her. At once she rushed headlong to him, opened her wings and embraced him tightly to her breast. Then she backed off a step or two and crouched.

The male, wings extended fully in the air above him, literally walked up her tail and stood on her back. The wings began to beat gently to balance him and he leaned forward and touched her neck softly with his beak, first on the left, then on the right. She trembled violently and her own wings raised to help balance his body. She tilted her head backwards toward him and the tip of his beak softly rubbed the base of hers. With that her head plunged forward and down and her tail rose high and the fluttering of the yearling increased as copulation commenced. During this act both birds gave voice to a repeated very light cooing similar to that made by the mourning dove.

In less than one minute the mating was completed and the male hopped lightly to the ground. Both birds uttered a series of meaningful clucks followed by the hen's gently pecking at his head several times in a gesture unmistakably one of pride at having been captivated by so strong and handsome a bird as he.

The unnerving din throughout the nesting area continued unabated around them, and during the remainder of that day and the two days which followed, while more pigeons were constantly arriving and participating in their own courtship, the pairing of birds everywhere became quite obvious.

Usually with the yearling male leading, the two would fly high and circle the area, plunge downward in steep dives, shoot in and out of the woods with reckless abandon and entirely give themselves up to the sheer joy of flying. At intervals as they settled to rest a stray unmated male might appear, but neither the yearling nor his mate permitted him to tarry too long in their vicinity.

Each time they came to rest the male sought out the firm branch of a tree and inspected it with a critical eye. During the second day he returned four times to the same crotch, eighteen feet high in a jack pine, and during the third day he landed nowhere else. The hen inspected his choice carefully and showed her approval by straddling the two branches which formed it.

Since the same activity was being engaged in by the vast majority of the other birds, very soon all of the crotches, especially those most favored near the trunk of the tree, were taken. None of those seeking a nesting site made any attempt to claim the crotch selected by the yearling and his mate. In some indefinable way it had become marked as their property and thus remained inviolate.

On the morning of the fourth day, after a bit of preliminary caressing and cooing, the yearling male set about finding nest-building material. The exuberance of the courtship concluded, the woods seemed almost peacefully quiet. At first there were plenty of twigs on the ground in the nearby vicinity but, since they were in unusual demand by this horde of nest-builders, the supply diminished apace and it became necessary to range ever farther afield to find them. For dozens of miles in all directions, the ground was as clear of twigs as if it had been swept.

Whenever he found a stick that suited him, the yearling gripped it crosswise in his bill and brought it back to the female in the jack pine. At first these were rather coarse twigs five to eight inches in length and a quarter-inch thick. As the hen lay the foundation for the nesting platform and skillfully wove the sticks together, the sticks needed became progressively smaller.

She was a good builder, this hen, and the nest quickly assumed the shape of a saucer with a diameter of eleven inches. As she built the nest higher she maintained a slight depression in the center and by the time the platform was two inches thick, the twigs being brought by the male were only a few inches long and quite slender.

For three days they worked on this construction together, pausing only rarely to reenact their copulation. Late in the afternoon of that third day she refused the final twig he had brought, signifying completion of the nest. Without wasted time she positioned herself erectly on this platform while the yearling male perched on the branch at her side and looked around contentedly at the great mass of nesting birds surrounding them.

The precision with which the flock's nesting colony was laid out was amazing, for its edges were as straight and true as if they had been measured with engineering equipment. The leading edge of the nesting area — where the yearling passenger pigeon and his mate had built their nest — was five miles wide and began exactly on the south bank of the Spirit River. Not one pair of passengers flew across this river to nest. From this front the area stretched back in a southeasterly direction for seventeen miles, encompassing the whole of the Newwood River from its spring origin just a couple of miles from the Spirit until it emptied into the Wisconsin six miles above Merrill.

In this perfectly rectangular area of five by seventeen miles, every bush and every tree without exception had its complement of nests; often as many as twelve dozen nests in a single larger tree and as few as two or three in the eight-foot high scrub oak and birch saplings.

So straight and precisely observed were the lines of this nesting area that where the line bisected a tree, the side of the tree inside the area would have dozens of nests, while that on the outside had none. No nest was lower than five feet nor higher than sixty-five feet. And from as far distant as five miles away in any direction from the edges of the colony, the loud and confused buzz of cooing, twittering, fluttering birds could be heard day and night.

It was a tremendous nesting, to be sure, but by no means the largest or even nearly the largest this state or other states had seen in the past. In the earlier years of this century nestings of from three to eight miles in width and up to one hundred miles in length had occurred, and even as short a time as five years ago nestings ten miles wide and forty miles long had been made. The yearling's hen herself had nested last season in Oklahoma in an area covered by passenger pigeons for fifteen miles in width and twenty in length. And so, while not the largest of record, this nesting was certainly of respectable size. Passenger pigeons were never really comfortable unless tightly crowded among their fellows.

The female sat motionless for two hours after completion of the nest and then stood high and raised her tail as a milk white egg dropped from her into the depression of the platform.

A bubbling, excited clucking sound came from her, and as if this were a signal he'd been waiting for, the yearling echoed it and flung himself outward and up. High he climbed and higher yet, executing the maneuvers he had learned from the almost forgotten dark male. He dived and spun, rolled and cartwheeled limply and before long the sky above this great stretch of swampy forest land was alive with madly wheeling male pigeons.

One of the instigators of this odd aerial display, the yearling was one of the first to cease his gyrations and bullet away to the southwest, followed by no less than ten thousand others. Similar groups sailed off in various directions in increased numbers and still the air above the nesting colony grew all the more crowded.

For forty minutes the yearling's flock flew. In the waning hours of daylight they circled a woods rich with birch and oak and settled to feed. When their crops were gorged with acorns they flew to a nearby alder swamp and here they roosted close together and content. So heavily cloaked were these little trees with the birds that from a short distance away it looked quite like these were dozens upon dozens of strangely misplaced haystacks rather than trees holding a punishing weight of passenger pigeons.

At intervals during the balmy night the yearling awoke briefly. The stars were brilliant chips scattered across the moonless heavens and even the lonesome wavering cry of a screech owl far in the distance sounded innocuous to him. He felt comfortable and at peace with the world and the closeness of the other roosting males created an aura of security. He murmured softly to himself and the sound seemed to carry an underlying note of pride and satisfaction.

He slept.

9

THE yearling passenger pigeon and his mate alternated in the incubation of this single egg of theirs in which they evidenced so much pride. It was a very precise process executed with the utmost care and steadfastness and it began in the morning after the laying of the egg.

The young bird's flock, after leaving its own roost at dawn to join an even larger flock of males passing overhead, flew with them to an oak forest where for an hour they scrabbled through leaves and underbrush with that highly effective rolling cylinder action, seeking out and devouring the delectable acorns.

Mostly the acorns they consumed were from the Hill's oak, for these were the hardest and best weathered the winter cold and spring moisture. Also in plentiful supply and in relatively good condition were the acorns of the scarlet, black and red oaks. There were plenty of white oaks and bur oaks in this region, both species of which had borne numerous acorns last fall, too, but those from the white oak germinated very rapidly after dropping and the extremely abundant bur oak acorns became spongy and usually rotted immediately after thawing.

After feeding, the birds perched in the oaks and slept with

their bills cushioned neatly on their swollen crops and nearly lost in the downy feathers. Then they took to the air and flew to a nearby creek where they lined the bank shoulder to shoulder on both sides of the watercourse for over two miles. After drinking deeply they headed back for the nesting colony.

As they flew they joined, and were joined by, many more flights of pigeons, and when they came within sight of their goal it was ten o'clock and the sky was black with birds from horizon to horizon, appearing for all the world like some great plague of locusts approaching. The nearer they came the more levelly they flew in carefully maintained layers but at different altitudes. These layers merged constantly until tier after tier of birds filled the air from as low as thirty feet to as high as four hundred and the noise of their coming was the roaring of a Niagara.

They decreased speed over the nesting area and plummeted in by the tens of thousands. How, in this area of millions of nests, it was possible for the individual male to locate his nest and mate was a mystery, and yet each bird knew its own area, its own tree, its own nest beyond any doubt and sped to it straightaway.

The yearling flashed down above the winding Spirit River and shot through the branches at blinding speed and with that unparalleled skill he had learned at the tail of the dark leader in the Canadian wilds. When he was only six feet from his nest his wings cupped the air and his tail flared widely and he came to a perfect stop at exactly the moment he reached the platform.

The beautiful hen had been waiting patiently on their egg, and though she did not look back at him as he approached her from the rear, she plunged from the nest a fraction of a second before he got there and by the time he had settled himself over the smooth warm egg she was flying with a milling mass of females close to the forest floor. The egg had been uncovered for no more than ten seconds.

In less than three minutes all the males had landed and taken over the duties of incubation and just that quickly the entire body of females climbed through the trees, gathered above them and set off in a rapidly dispersing cloud for distant feeding places. The thunder of their departure diminished and then the air was still, and not a flying bird could be seen.

The yearling snuggled comfortably on the platform, enclosing the egg in the billowy feathers of his underside, and forthwith went to sleep. A time or two during the day he awakened and turned the egg with his bill, shifted his own position a bit and settled down again.

It was going on three o'clock in the afternoon before he became truly alert again. Although the woods were still he cocked his head this way and that and, as if on cue, the sound came. It was a barely audible murmur that might easily have been mistaken for a distant breeze in the foliage, but it steadily increased in volume to a loud rustling, a rising storm, a frightful thundering of wings. The females were returning and the action they executed now was similar to his own of the morning.

The female approached from behind and he identified her

wingbeats among the hundreds of others nearby when she was still twenty feet from him. He did not look back toward her, but at the slight popping noise of her braking action he braced himself and hurtled from the nest.

With some fifty thousand males he flew to the north. They crossed over several dirt roads and one major highway and each time they did so guns barked and birds fell. Though they were in a basically unsettled area, there was an abnormally large number of wagons and horses on these roads and the young bird felt distinctly uneasy. Men and wagons had always foretokened disaster for his species. The losses through such random firing were light, and the flock continued at the same mile-eating pace. Approximately fifty miles from the nesting area it circled and landed in a woods through which wound the Flambeau River.

After feeding and resting they flew south and found that the roads were even more heavily traveled than before, and at the rail lines in Tripoli and Tomahawk there was unusual activity, with regular streams of barrel-laden wagons pulling away.

The male passenger pigeons had returned to the vicinity of the nesting colony from all points of the compass and now, instead of returning to the nests, they formed five different roosts. One of these was between Tomahawk and the colony and another east of the Wisconsin River by Tug Lake. Two were southwest of the nesting area — one at the headwaters of the Copper River and the other along the Big Rib River. The final one, and farthest away, was along the banks of the Wisconsin River midway between Merrill and Wausau. In each of these roosts there were approximately eighty million passenger pigeons . . . all males. They perched side by side on every limb of every tree for miles and here they remained each night thereafter of the nesting period.

At other roosts and nesting colonies similar to these — located in Michigan and Pennsylvania, Ohio and Indiana and Kentucky — men with their horses and wagons were converging. For days the telegraph wires east of the Mississippi and north of the Mason-Dixon Line had hummed with news of their locations and populations, and now came the professional bird hunters and netters. From Chicago and Milwaukee and Madison they came on train by the hundreds to Wausau and Merrill and Tomahawk, and from Cleveland and Detroit, Pittsburgh, Indianapolis, Louisville and Cincinnati they hastened to other nestings and other roosts.

The passenger pigeons were money — big money — for the man who knew his trade. A good netter with an experienced crew of helpers could capture upwards of twenty to fifty barrels of birds per day and, at three hundred birds per barrel that was a gold mine. A single barrel of beheaded and gutted birds, iced down and shipped to Chicago, brought twenty-five dollars, and those taken alive for trapshooting could be sold right on the spot for twenty-five cents per dozen, and double that in crates aboard boxcars in Wausau. And the best part of it all was that the prices were rising every year. It used to be that when the birds were in greater numbers they brought two or three cents each, sometimes only a penny apiece, but for the trapper, things had certainly changed for the better. The birds weren't in such wholly unbelievable numbers anymore and with so many uses being found for the fool birds, the demand was greater.

Because a man could earn a year's wages in five weeks of concerted work and just take life easy the rest of the year, the business was highly attractive. Everything about the birds could be sold in one form or another. Why, the most uninformed person knew that dried gizzards of passenger pigeons stewed in milk was a sure cure for gallstones, and so hundreds of thousands of the birds were slain for their gizzards alone.

And even if you weren't a very good bird netter yourself or didn't have the necessary equipment, a small fortune lay on the ground where the netters gutted their market birds, because it was a simple fact of life that the stomach of the bird, dried and then pulverized into powder and mixed with a little whiskey and water would clear up the bloody fluxes in no time. And even if it didn't, the cheap whiskey it was blended with created a rosy glow for awhile and made the partaker *think* he felt better. This was a concoction particularly favored by those who would not have considered entering a tavern to buy spirits.

And the dung! Now there was the money-maker. Rich in saltpeter for making explosives and excellent as a fertilizer, it was also a natural medicine. Better than snake oil, easier to get and process. There just wasn't any malady of man nor beast it wouldn't ease. Dried, crushed and mixed with molasses it was a sure-fire remedy for migraine and all other forms of headaches. Stomachaches vanished when it was taken, and the devastating effects of pleurisy and colic, dysentery and apoplexy simply vanished after a spoonful or two. And if you were healthy to begin with, it was even highly recommended as a deterrent to lethargy and spring fever. Yes sir, better by far than any ridiculous snake oil cure-all.

Suffering from weak eyes? Your troubles were over with the purchase of a bottle of pigeon blood eye-easer. A bucket of freshly drawn pigeon blood mixed with a hundred gallons of water made a pinkish solution absolutely guaranteed to ease eyestrain, cure sties, halt and even improve failing sight and, on occasion, it could miraculously restore sight to the blind!

And, friend, if you've never slept beneath a feather tick stuffed with the soft breast down of passenger pigeon, you've just never slept comfortably. It only took a thousand or so birds to make one and, naturally, the price was high, but it was worth every penny if you valued your night's rest. And how the hogs loved the unused carcasses!

But these were just some of the side benefits of the booming business of pigeon slaughtering. The two principal sources of income were in the dressed-down carcasses for meat and live birds for sport.

The meat was delicious, some folks said. Of course, there were those who claimed they'd rather eat boiled crow than the dry, tough, dark, stringy meat of the adult passenger pigeon, but then you can't please everyone, and not all folks could afford choice steaks and roasts and chops. And if you took care with the preparation, it really wasn't too bad at all. And the best part, there wasn't a cheaper meat to be had on the market, nor one that could be fixed in so many different ways.

It could be sun-dried or smoked, broiled or baked, roasted, stewed or fried and it even made a passable jerky. You could pickle it in kegs of brine or preserve it in great crocks of spiced apple cider and you could even can them whole, one or two to the quart jar.

For sport there was nothing better, no doubt about it. Trap-shooting had become one of the most popular pastimes of the age and, true to be told, the passenger pigeon bursting from confinement and frantically flying away made a very satisfactory target. Of course, the bird seldom got away. It was a rich man's sport, this trapshooting. Above and beyond the cost of shells and club memberships, each bird released cost the gunner thirty cents. The common gentry couldn't very well afford such expensive entertainment, but many cashed in on it anyway. If the sportsman missed his shot there was always an encircling ring of armed spectators too poor to join a trap-shooting club themselves, who delighted in throwing up a barrage through which only the most incredibly lucky of birds might fly unscathed.

Above all, there was no need to worry about wiping out the species. How could you destroy a species which swept across the sky in flocks numbering in the hundreds of millions, even billions? No sir, the passenger pigeon would be around forever and there was hardly a more lucrative business that a young man could aspire to learn than pigeon netting or shooting.

Learn they did, too. Where in the early part of the 1800's professional hunters and netters numbered in the low hundreds, by the mid-1880's they numbered in the thousands, and there were hundreds of devices for taking the birds dead or alive and each year these devices were perfected or new ones invented.

Just a few years ago in Grand Traverse County, Michigan, at a tremendous nesting site, a mere handful of men had become wealthy indeed when in a matter of three weeks they furnished for the market over five million passenger pigeons, of which slightly more than half were plump squabs. Other hunters at the same place did nearly as well and this was an inspiration indeed to those who liked the idea of getting rich quick.

For every major flight of pigeons that moved anywhere east of the Rockies, the wires would buzz with news of their passage, and any place the birds remained for more than four days was very apt to become a death trap.

So it was now, in this remote swampy wilderness of Wisconsin, that the men came. They brought barrels by the thousands and horses and wagons by the hundreds. Their nets and cages and clubs alone filled dozens of wagons and the guns and ammunition they brought were sufficient for starting a major revolution.

But still, day after day, the adult passengers were not molested anywhere near the nesting areas, for these men had grown wise in the ways of the big wild pigeon. If disrupted before the eggs hatched, they were very apt to desert their nests and fly great distances to another location to begin the nesting cycle anew, leaving only the unhatched eggs behind.

With squabs in the nests, however, they would remain. A great deal of money had been lost by hunters before they learned this lesson, and so now they bided their time. As long as the birds weren't too badly disturbed they wouldn't leave, and so even though each hunter and netter was competition for the next man, they all entered into something of a pact with one another to leave the roosts and the nesting area alone until the time was right.

It didn't take long for the time to become right, either, because of all known pigeon species in the world, the incubation period of the passenger pigeon was shortest. And so, for thirteen days the eggs were incubated and the males and females continued to spell one another in the task at specific times in morning and evening. They were not shot or otherwise molested within miles of the nesting area, but elsewhere they were not so safe.

While this nesting colony was large, to be sure, it still did not take long for enterprising hunters and netters to stake out their positions along the perimeter and prepare their equipment. Those who arrived too late to establish a claim were forced to head out to the feeding areas surrounding the colony fifty miles in all directions, but even they were not so unfortunate. The birds had to eat and it wasn't difficult to determine where a particular flock would land next time, and so these latecomers strung their great nets and set their traps and staged their ambushes.

Seldom a day passed that they did not have some degree of luck. A huge seine one hundred yards long could be stretched across a river or creek, and almost invariably during the day one flight or another of the pigeons following the watercourse low to the water would ram into it, piling one into another until hundreds, sometimes thousands, fell dead or injured to the water and were picked up by boats several hundred yards downstream.

Great purse nets, too, were strung between treeless avenues of the forests, for it was in these open places with trees on both sides of them that the pigeons liked to skim along only six or eight feet above the ground. The purse net was an extremely effective device. Like a filmy windsock held open for its full length, it seemed at the entrance innocuous to the birds, and they sped into it, only to be forced closer and closer together as the cone narrowed and finally to fall in a great scrambling mass to the earth, where men and boys would rush out to grasp each head projecting through the mesh and snip it off with their blacksmith pincers.

Box traps were used with figure-four triggers, baited with acorns or heavily salted corn kernels, but such devices seldom took more than two or three dozen birds at a time and, except by the smallest of operators, were considered a waste of time.

Most treacherous of all, perhaps, was the device which very nearly ended the young passenger pigeon's existence. For ten days now he and his mate had been incubating their egg, and on his morning flight to a feeding ground near Chippewa Falls with several thousand other males he spied a bog area where the black mud actually glistened with the startling white of salt. Very faintly from down there they heard the feeding cry of their own kind and immediately they turned, circled and then began to settle in the surrounding trees. A handful of pigeons were already on the ground there, not eating but simply sitting on the crust of mud as if having already eaten their fill and resting.

They seemed suspiciously still to the yearling as he continued to circle with the majority of the flock, but what little fear nagged him was allayed when, near the edge of the bog and not far from an unusually large tangle of branches and sedge grasses, a solitary male passenger pigeon flapped his wings excitedly and again the feeding call came to them reassuringly; a long drawn-out and moderately loud repetition of one note rendered in a squeaky voice.

The birds still in the air and those already settled in the trees answered in chorus with a harsh, low sound very similar to the quacking of a duck. Not one of the pigeons seemed to detect that the feeding call they heard did not, in fact, come from this flapping male. Nor did they notice that the eyelids of this bird had been sewn shut and that his feet were securely strapped to a tilted stick held at an angle by another stick firmly embedded in the mud.

The job this male bird was performing was not, of course, of his own choosing. He had been trapped some days ago for just this purpose and the stool for him to sit upon on the edge of this bog baited with fresh salt was clever indeed.

This was the stool pigeon and, in a later day, the term would be used freely for describing unsavory individuals who through deceit led or talked their fellows into trouble.

Blindly he perched at the projecting end of his stool stick with the other, heavier end touching the ground. A long cord attached to this end ran to the tangle of branches and grasses where six men, cleverly camouflaged, crouched with their guns at ready.

When the yearling's flock began to settle to the nearby trees, one of the men pulled the cord. This raised the grounded end of the "stool" and caused the end with the pigeon on it to dip sharply. At the sensation of falling, the bird instinctively thrust out his wings and fluttered to maintain his balance, and it was this movement of the live decoy bird that convinced the flock they had nothing to fear here. If there was danger, one of their own kind would not be down there carelessly fluttering while others apparently dozed in the sun nearby.

Descending in their usual dense funnel shape, the birds began to alight and peck avidly at the salt. The yearling was among the first few to land and as he felt an alien cord mesh beneath his feet he sensed something terribly wrong. Alarm screeched from him and was echoed by the others but it was too late. Another rope in the pigeon blind was yanked and the opposing wings of a huge butterfly-shaped net leaped from the ground and effectively snapped shut over the yearling and more than a thousand other males.

A chorus of frantic grunt-like chirpings arose, interspersed with the continued sharp tweets of danger, as this net flopped to the ground with its struggling quarry. The birds not ensnared abruptly changed direction and began to speed away, but now the shotguns barked time and again and a rain of pigeons tumbled to the ground.

The frantic strugglings of the birds caught in the net caused an ill-repaired section to burst near the yearling, freeing him and a score of others. Swiftly the freed birds took wing and behind them the men cursed and tossed their empty guns aside as they scrambled to pounce on the net and seal the gap.

Far, far ahead the escapees spotted the remainder of their flock speeding away and they barreled after them as fast as they could fly. Meanwhile, the male stool pigeon back at the salt-baited bog trembled violently as the cries of the trapped birds and the gunfire smote his ears, and he tore at his stitched eyelids with his wings.

The men wasted no time in silencing this tumult. As the proud blue heads of the males poked through the mesh they grabbed them in the fork of index and middle fingers, palm up, placed the ball of the thumb atop the head and pressed until the skull crushed. It was faster, they had found, to do this than to use pincers and there was less likelihood of damaging the net.

When the trapped birds had all been killed, the net was opened and they were hurriedly tossed into sacks and carried into hiding behind the blind. The net was placed, its trigger reset and the mesh on the ground disguised with a scattering of dead grasses. A new supply of fresh white salt was spread and a dozen dead birds were propped into squatting positions here and there to act as decoys.

One of the men checked the stool pigeon and found that the bird's exertions had ripped one of his eyelids apart. He grunted angrily and slogged back to the blind.

A moment later he returned with needle and thread and, with the skill of considerable practice, he pushed it through the tattered and bleeding eyelid and resealed it. Then he hustled back to the blind where the other men were busy reloading their weapons or cleaning the birds. He was just in time, for one of the men grabbed his arm and pointed. He looked, nodded and quickly took a little reed device from his pocket and blew through it a series of enticing feeding cries.

In the distance a dark smudge in the sky heralded the approach of another contingent of males.

10

A̲ᴛ precisely 11:22 A.M. on the thirteenth day after the
beautiful female had laid her single egg, the yearling
passenger pigeon's first offspring hatched.

It was a female, wet and helpless, covered with a motley
few hairlike strands of yellow feathering plastered to its sides,
and its great bulging eyes were all but covered by blue-black
lids. She was unspeakably ugly, but to the young passenger
pigeon and his mate she was the most wonderful thing in the
world, and from that instant on there was nothing so important in the world as her safekeeping.

For others of their neighbors, however, there was to be no
such joy. In their own jack pine alone, in which there had
been fifty-four nesting pairs of birds, three eggs lay abandoned
because one or both of the parents had been destroyed. Nesting platforms that were to have become cradles had instead
become biers.

The yearling passenger pigeon's mate had not left the nest
that morning when he returned from feeding and so very little
milk had formed in her crop. What was there she gave to her
chick immediately after flicking the eggshell halves from the
nest. Very tenderly she maneuvered the tiny head into her

mouth and then regurgitated the thick nutritious white fluid into the hatchling's mouth. The little bird's capacity was slight and so, even though her mother had little to offer at once, it was more than enough. The female left right after that and the yearling took her place, carefully straddling the tiny bird and snuggling down upon her so that she was warm and safe.

That this same hatching process was occurring in the other nests became quite evident, not only because the ground below became liberally strewn with eggshells but because the routine of the adults was broken for the first time since the eggs had been laid. Instinctively knowing their eggs would be hatching soon, the females had steadfastly refused to leave their nests when the males returned until the young came forth and were fed by them. As a result, instead of the hens leaving all at the same time as had been the custom, now there was a continuous but more sparsely numbered exodus and it was well over three hours after the yearling's mate's departure that the last of the other females disappeared from view.

A vague memory of his own parents came to the young passenger pigeon as he arched his neck around to feed the tiny bird that was a part of him, and a comforting and over-powering protectiveness engulfed him for this little spark of life.

The chick ate eagerly and frequently, and by the time the female returned, about four in the afternoon, he had fed her five times and his crop was nearly empty. He heard his mate coming and this time he did not leap from the nest and fly away, but flitted to the branch beside it and watched as she

landed gently on the edge of the nest and snuggled over the
baby until only the tip of its beak projected from her breast
feathers. After a slight pause she began to feed it from her
own now copiously filled crop and the yearling murmured a
low note of approval and vaulted into the air.

By the following day something of a routine had been re-
established, with males and females spelling each other on the
nests, although now the intervals were shorter. The males still
roosted away from the nesting area while the females covered
the chicks all night. By eight in the morning the males had fed
and watered and returned to the nests and the females left,
only themselves to return with their crops full less than four
hours later. At three o'clock there was another change and just
before sunset the males were relieved for the remainder of the
night.

The reason for the adults' earlier wanderings of as much as
fifty or sixty miles away from the nesting area for food during
the incubation period was now revealed. The little birds
seemed to grow visibly with each feeding and each time a
little more food was taken than at the preceding meal. It became necessary to feed them more often and to do so the
adults were obliged to spend less time traveling after food.
Thus, their feeding excursions took them only ten or fifteen
or twenty-five miles from the nest, to areas of plentiful food
supply which they had previously ignored.

At the end of the sixth day the baby female was sitting
erect well enough by herself and a downy feathering was
effectively hiding the yellow egg feathers. Already the nest-

ling had more than trebled its size, and its demands for food were constant and taxed the parents to their utmost.

The milk she received now was heavy with thick curd and little whole seeds were mixed with it. She thrived on the food and demanded ever more and the forest was in a constant state of uproar with the peepings of the young and the thunderous comings and goings of the adults.

It was on the seventh dawn after the hatching that the men moved in.

They worked systematically, these eight hundred or so men, each going about his business without too much concern for the others. Conversation was out of the question, for only when a man shouted into his companion's ear could he make himself understood over the din.

They wore slickers and boots, old clothing and wide-brimmed hats, and they toted pouches stuffed with three-bushel sacks. Before entering the woods each securely attached one of these sacks to his waist.

The females showed no fear of these men moving about and even when the bird in a neighboring nest was grabbed about the middle of the back to pin her wings, and her head and crop were popped off with one savage jerk, they showed little concern and their bright orange-red eyes stared steadily at the intruders.

The low nests were the first to be assaulted; and these were everywhere between five and seven feet high by the tens of thousands. A man working hard and fast soon established a rhythm — step, reach, grab, retract, yank, drop, stuff in sack —

and a bird in the bag every five seconds, a dozen birds per minute, was an extremely good pace. But arms grow weary and fingers ripping off heads and crops become sore and the fires of initial enthusiasm wane somewhat and so, by the time the male passenger pigeons arrived shortly after eight o'clock, the carnage had reduced to five or fewer birds per minute for each man.

The males paid no more attention to the men than had the females, and as the hens left the nests they positioned themselves over the squabs and fed them as usual. And now the men began to grumble among themselves, for their work had suddenly become messier and more distasteful. The crops of the males were very full and the yank given to pop off head and crop resulted in the crop bursting and its contents spraying over the men, greasing their hands and dripping down their slickers and making the dung-coated ground slick and treacherous.

And while the guano itself had made the aroma of the woods far from pleasant before, now the stench of the curdled crop milk rose about them in a nauseous gas which sickened more than one man and purged their insides with violent upheavals.

The ground behind each man became a scene from some fearful room of Hell as the more brightly colored heads of the males attached to their crops were cast aside amid wafting feathers and the sprinkling of curds and milk and blood in a hideous montage.

Each of the bags the men carried was capable of holding

from seventy-five to one hundred carcasses, and as each was filled the mouth was firmly tied with rough rope and labeled with the hunter's tag and propped against a tree for later pickup.

At approximately noon the men from opposing sides of the nesting area met in the middle and paused in their labors to shout plaintively in one another's ears about how hard they had worked. They dug from their deep pockets sandwiches wrapped in paper, which they ate while squatting with their backs against trees. And when they had finished with their food and their pipes, another change of shifts in the birds had taken place. The females had returned, and the men started back over practically the same ground previously covered. From each nest where a male had been taken before, now a female was removed and slaughtered. And when, in mid-afternoon, they reached the point where the first change of shift among the birds had taken place — obvious because of the change in coloration of the heads on the ground — they waited, smoking, until the great roaring came again and the shift was changed a final time, and now once more the heads of the males joined those of their mates already scattered profanely beneath the nests.

Of all this, the yearling passenger pigeon and his mate knew nothing on the first day or even on the second or third, because the onslaught had begun many miles southeast of them in that final five miles of the great nesting area which bordered the Wisconsin River above Merrill. But their own area was not sacrosanct.

The eight hundred men had covered the initial twenty-five square miles with reasonable thoroughness, and few were the low nests they had missed. It was full dusk by the time they had finished the first day's slaughter, but their work was not yet finished. With the light of their lanterns they returned along their paths time and again to carry out of the woods the sacks of birds they had filled.

There was an average of seven full bags for each of these men, and not until many hours after darkness had fallen were the last of the birds transported to the river and there loaded aboard huge rafts to be floated to the landing near Merrill, where they would be salted or iced down in huge barrels and shipped to Milwaukee and Chicago.

And when, at last, the hunters slid under their blankets beneath the stars in their various camps, they were bone weary, and only a few of them found sleep elusive and lay awake long enough to consider the significance of the rising chorus of pitiable peepings that came from this area of the woods.

This chorus was the lament of a quarter million squabs which shivered in the cool night air and whose bellies ached with the lack of food and whose parents would return no more. Hardly the size of a blackbird and too small yet to be marketable themselves, these baby birds had been left in their nests to await an end which, if somewhat slower and less violent than that suffered by their parents, was no less certain or terrible.

Although not too many of the men paid any attention to this strange, heartbreaking chorus, a few of them did. For them it was more than just a thunder of peepings. For them it was a dirge they would remember all the rest of their lives. On those lonely nights in years hence when sleep eluded them again, the refrain would return with the low moaning of the wind in a haunting whisper in the darkness and they would suddenly know an abysmal guilt.

The next morning the onslaught was resumed and during that day another five miles of the nesting area was stripped of its low-nesting birds. The day after that a similar area followed. But by the end of this third day of the hunt it was noted that the adults were spending considerably less time at their nests during the day and that in five more days they would be abandoning their young naturally. If the hunters were to get a good showing of adult birds in their bags, they would have to step up their activities. With this goal in mind the hunters worked longer hours, especially by lantern light, since the females, at least, still remained on their nests at night to protect their squabs from the cold air. The leaders of the hunting groups sent emissaries to Tomahawk and Merrill and Wausau to recruit more help and the pace of the slaughter increased.

When the yearling passenger pigeon returned to his nest after the morning feeding the next day — which was the tenth day after the squab had hatched — the ground below his jack pine was strewn with loose feathers and heads with crops still attached to them, and in the air there was the odor of fear and death, and the yearling became nervous.

His little squab was now reasonably well feathered and

gaining a degree of attractiveness. Her yellow hair feathers still projected here and there through the overall brown and gave the fledgling a rather comical unfinished appearance, as if she had been knit of threads and the trailing ends of many ties had not yet been trimmed away. At this stage of her development she weighed as much as her mother, but since she had virtually no tail feathers and only partially developed pinions, she was awkward and unbalanced. When she tried to stand high, she constantly tipped forward onto her beak or far back onto her sparsely feathered rump.

Although the yearling passenger pigeon's mate stayed with the fledgling throughout each night and would continue to do so for at least two more nights to come, both she and the male spent much less time at the nest during the daylight hours. Though neither of them would stay away for very long — ordinarily not over an hour — their stays at the nest were brief. This was essentially because the fledgling female had grown large enough to take in a single feeding the entire contents of the crop of one of its parents. Only a very little curd remained in the crops of the adults, and the foodstuffs given to the squab were mostly partially softened acorns and seeds and the buds of various trees. So greedy had the little one become, in fact, that she kept both parents continually on the go for food.

Other fledglings in nearby nests were not faring quite so well as she. Many of them had lost one or the other of their parents in nets or ambushes as they had gone out to feed or collect food for the squab. As a result, with only one parent to carry the load of providing enough food the fledglings were not getting enough to eat and were thin and weaker than they should have been.

On the twelfth day the pattern of the hunt changed and the men began swiftly working their way back from this head of the nesting area to its foot along the Wisconsin River. It would seem that the epitome of bestiality had already been reached here in the slaughter of low-nesting birds, but now the awful carnage became even more fearsome and wantonly destructive.

The yearling had just returned to the nest and was feeding his squab when they came, and he quickly crouched protectively over the youngster, although this in itself was no easy task since she had grown so large. He watched them come, and some of the men were armed with poles ten feet long with a knob at the outstretched end. They worked in pairs, one of them using the pole to strike, if possible, adult birds sitting on the nests. More often than not these blows were successful, but even when they were not and the adult managed to fly away, the next step was to give the nest a solid punch from below with the knob. This caused the nest to fly apart and knocked the squab into the air. Unable to fly even a little, the heavy squabs plummeted to the ground and hit solidly; so solidly, in fact, that frequently their fat bodies burst open like overripe tomatoes at the impact. The partners of the pole-wielders followed behind them picking up the birds so dislodged, ripping off heads and crops and thrusting both squabs and adults into the bags, for the squabs, now the size of big quail or even larger, had reached an acceptable size for marketing.

Occasionally one of the squabs that had split open upon

[149]

impact with the ground would be used as a projectile to be thrown at nesting platforms too high to be reached with the poles. The men were good shots and the squabs frequently hit their marks and knocked other squabs to the ground, much in the manner that apples tossed by little boys knock other, inaccessible apples from trees in the fall. And sometimes the injured squab being so used would remain alive for three or four such throws.

But it was when the men came to the birches that the greatest horror enveloped the yearling passenger pigeon. These were tall, spindly birches and their first branches were seldom within reach of the pole. Each, however, held many nests, about half of which were occupied by adult birds as well as squabs.

Each of these birches, forming fresh new bark beneath the old, was covered by a thin, loose papering of old bark. Scarcely thicker than writing paper, the bark was uniform over the trunk and all the branches and it was, unfortunately, extremely combustible.

At such trees the bag carrier would strike a match and touch it to the bark at the base. Immediately there would be a flash of almost explosive nature and the fire would race in an instant to every inch of the tree, bathing it in a fierce flame which lasted for at least a full minute.

With their plumage badly scorched, the adult birds would spring off the nests to fly away but, damaged too badly, would cartwheel to the ground, followed within seconds by their squabs as they scrambled out of their dry twig nests which had begun to burn. Often fifty or more birds could be taken in this manner from a single birch, and few were the white-barked trees which were passed by without being ignited.

The passenger pigeon residents of three big birches set afire within a radius of one hundred feet of the yearling's jack pine tumbled to their deaths and their carcasses filled one sack and part of another for the jubilant hunters.

When they came to his tree, the yearling crouched even lower over his squab and he could feel the vibrations as the pole knocked down a couple of dozen nests from the branches beneath him. His own nest, however, was just out of reach of the pole-wielder, and though that individual three times tossed squabs at him, a branch just beneath the one on which the yearling's nest was located deflected the living missile and the men moved off.

For more than an hour, even after the return of the female, the yearling remained protectively over the squab. The hunger of the little fledgling female made it squirm so badly, however, that he was forced to get up. He fed her what little remained in his crop and then moved to one side to let his mate feed the youngster what she had brought.

The handsome pair of adults preened their feathers for a short while and then took off together, climbed high above the woods and flew to the northeast with several thousand others. Behind them was a curious sight, for every few minutes there would come a billowing puff of blue-white smoke, at the base of which there would be a short-lived bright glow. And even when the woods itself had disappeared from view, the location of the nesting colony could be pinpointed immediately by the smoke signal–like puffs which rose high in the windless sky.

Actual shooting in the nesting area commenced on the thirteenth day, and over a thousand armed men roamed the eighty-five square miles of nesting area. They shot with abandon at any cluster of adult birds where enough could be downed with one shot to justify the expenditure of the shell. Most of these shooters considered less than ten birds per shot a distinct waste of time, effort and ammunition.

During that day the forest was a fantastic welter of sound, for adult birds flew constantly as they left to seek food for their young or returned with it, only to be shot at both going and coming. It was not until late in the afternoon that the guns were laid aside at last and the job of picking up the thousands and tens of thousands and hundreds of thousands of pigeon carcasses from the horribly befouled forest floor began.

This job stretched over many hours, and not even a quarter of the slain birds had been recovered when the men quit for the day, too exhausted to do more. After lying dead this many hours with heads and crops still attached, the meat wouldn't be much good anyway, and tomorrow, during the last return of the adults to the nests, they could bring down fresher meat. In the days after that they could concentrate solely on the squabs.

The yearling passenger pigeon and his mate were very fortunate. Though several times during the day various hunters had stalked by beneath their nest, they happened to be absent at these times and so escaped the explosive death which obliterated so many of the adults from neighboring nests.

The squab was left to herself on the thirteenth night while the yearling passenger pigeon and his mate roosted together miles away at a remote woods in which a half million of their species had gathered. When morning came this entire flock fed heavily, stuffing their crops as full as possible and then rising as one to fly in a rather leisurely manner back to their nests and young for the last time.

From various directions flocks similar in size to their own approached the colony an hour before noon, and the sky was darkened by them as they winged to their own nesting sites to deliver up the final feeding to the squabs. And when the sky over the nesting area was darkest with them, when many of the pigeons, including the yearling and his mate, had already landed and begun the feeding of their young, the greatest barrage of the fortnight-old assault began.

A thousand shotguns spoke simultaneously and in one instant's time over thirty thousand adults fell dead. The shooting continued more sporadically but without pause as the remainder of the flock poured in to fulfill their last duty here. Even when the adult birds were out of the air the firing went on, and adults and young alike were slain in the act of giving or receiving food.

The continuous shooting was highly distressing to the yearling passenger pigeon and his mate, but though they flinched frequently as the frightening boomings sounded from below and charges of fine pigeon shot ripped through the branches and into nests and birds, they continued their feeding without pause.

Their selection of this nesting site had been far more fortunate than they realized. The nest had been just too far above the ground in the initial by-hand onslaughts of the very low nests or even by the following pole-wielders. And now they were too low for the shooters whose aim was directed to the thickly nested areas closer to the treetops so that their shot charges could spread in larger patterns and thus down a greater number of birds.

As soon as the female had finished regurgitating the entire contents of her crop into the squab's eager mouth, the yearling passenger pigeon took over. And though the fledgling showed an inclination to stop feeding before his crop was half empty, he forced her to continue and packed the food in so tightly that by the time he had finished the little bird was scarcely able to raise herself.

Their job was finished now and they wasted no time in departing. As far as they were concerned the squab, from this moment on, had ceased to exist. Airborne, they zigzagged to a considerable height, leveled off and joined a small flock of passengers headed northward, never to return to this dangerous ground.

They flew with relative slowness, and continually more birds joined them. Soon the flock was a five-hundred-yard-wide ribbon trailing out behind for twenty miles or more. It had been a disastrous nesting on the whole and tens of millions of adults and fledglings had been slain — of which considerably less than half eventually found their way to market, the remainder being left to rot where they had fallen.

It was wonderful to be flying free again, with the onerous burden of nesting responsibilities lifted, and the birds chattered gutturally among themselves as they passed over the town of Minocqua.

The yearling passenger pigeon had left his mate to take a position in the lead of the flock and so he didn't even hear the single sharp crack of the rifle five hundred feet below. He didn't know that the lone bullet had torn through three birds and lodged in a fourth and that the four of them had tumbled.

Nor did he know that the last of the four to hit the ground was the beautiful female he had wooed and won.

II

THE fledgling female lay quietly on her platform eighteen feet up in the jack pine. The sound of gunfire had diminished considerably and at first her closed eyes had opened at intervals to scan the sky expectantly, but no adults flew up there as always before.

The trembling had long since ceased rippling through her fat little body and even most of the fear was gone now. With the gradual cessation of the shooting the sound that remained to fill the woods was a scrambled conglomeration of men's voices and cries from fledglings unfed and afraid. These sounds had continued so long that they just stopped having any meaning to her. The heavy pressure in her crop had become somewhat alleviated and she was more comfortable. Thus, worn out by the string of tragedies culminating in the great gunfire of earlier this day, she slept deeply and did not awaken until the small hand snatched her.

"Here's a big 'un," called a young voice to a man standing down below. "Looks to be in pretty good shape."

"Any busted feathers or shot-off toes?"

The boy inspected the fledgling carefully and shook his head. "Uh-huh."

"The beak whole?"

"Yep."

"Both eyes good?"

"Big an' bright."

"Craw good an' full?"

The boy squeezed the swollen crop and grinned at the man. "Like a cannonball."

"Okay, sack it up. That'll be enough, too. This one makes thirty-six we got now. Doc only asked for a couple dozen."

The boy nodded and stuffed the fledgling into a sack with several others and shinnied back down the tree carefully. The man took the bag from him and together they headed back to the town of Spirit Falls.

Strangely, there was little fear in the female fledgling. It was dark in the sack and though there was a prolonged jostling, it wasn't unbearable. She was even able to continue her napping in a rather fitful manner.

Some time later she was aware that movement had ceased and that there was a harsh hammering close by which came at intervals and the sound of a man's deep voice, humming to himself. Shortly after the hammering stopped the bag was lifted. Light showed momentarily at the neck of the bag as a hand reached in, brushed by her and closed over the form of one of the birds beside her. This bird was lifted out and in a moment the hand returned. This time she was the one picked up and she struggled briefly, but the grip was tight and so she relaxed.

The light came from a pair of kerosene lanterns sitting on

a bench and she had time only to see that she was in a large rough-hewn room with several bulging sacks on the floor. Then she was carefully positioned in a newly constructed crate and the lid closed above her.

The crate was two feet wide by three and a half feet long and it was only five inches high. One after another the birds were stuffed into this box in three rows — twelve (including the female squab) with their heads to one side, twelve with their heads to the other side and the final twelve rather roughly squeezed into the slot that had formed in the middle of the crate. Needless to say, there was little room for movement. Even crouched on their breasts, the tops of the birds' heads and their backs rubbed the lid of the crate.

Actually, this crowding was not too unlike that the squabs had been accustomed to when their parents had crouched above them in the nests. For a little while it even provided something of a sense of security to the captives.

The box was lifted and carried outside and placed in a wagon which, in turn, transported the birds to a depot. Within the hour, high on a stack of boxes in a baggage car, they began a long swaying journey over clicking rails.

For some thirty hours they alternately moved and stopped. The relative comfort of the crowding had quickly become discomfort and then pain. Several of the birds cried out despairingly and struggled frantically against this bondage and five of those in the center row succeeded in turning themselves upside down, where they lay pinned.

When the movement finally ceased, eight of the inner birds

were dead and two others were dying, smothered by the feathers of their companions. Only those two on the opposite ends of the middle row where a little fresh air had been able to seep in managed to survive the journey. The young female had been most fortunate in her position in an outer row where a good supply of fresh air entered through a crack in the wood, but her crop was empty and she was ravenous and her muscles ached constantly from the cramping.

The box was lifted and placed into a wagon which then rattled and bumped along for better than forty-five minutes before stopping.

"You the boss here?" the deliveryman asked.

S. A. Stephan, general manager of the Cincinnati Zoological Gardens, looked up and nodded.

"Box here for you. C.O.D. Live birds, it says."

Stephan paid the charges and carried the crate to the aviary. He beckoned to another man and they entered a wire mesh cage ten feet square.

"Crazy way to ship live birds," said the second man. "I wouldn't bet they'll be alive, would you?"

Stephan grunted noncommittally and opened the door of the crate, which had been wired shut. His hand groped inside and closed gently over the back of the female fledgling and he drew her out carefully.

"Female," he said. "Not in bad shape, considering. I think she'll make it."

He stretched out one of her legs with his free hand and his assistant put a small metal band with a number on it around

her shin and cautiously squeezed it closed with a pair of pliers.
He noted the number in a small leather-covered binder.

"Our first female passenger pigeon," he remarked. He looked
up and smiled at the manager. "Since she's our first lady,
maybe we ought to name her after the First Lady of the
nation."

Stephan shook his head. "That might not go over too well.
But there's no reason why we couldn't name her after the
very first First Lady, Martha Washington."

The assistant nodded and jotted the name down beside the
leg band number. "Martha it is," he said.

Stephan released her then and she scrambled across the floor
to a far corner where she cowered as the two men continued
banding, recording and releasing the birds.

The two birds that had been dying had finally succumbed,
and the manager set them and the other eight dead birds to
the side to be skinned or mounted.

"You know," he said sadly, "it's just criminal to pack living
creatures together like that. It's just a wonder to me that
more of them weren't dead."

His assistant agreed and then stood up and shut his book.
"Mr. Stephan," he said seriously, "do you really believe like
you said before that the passenger pigeons are in danger of
becoming extinct? I don't doubt your word," he said hurriedly, "but, I don't know, it just doesn't seem probable or even
possible that with all the millions and millions of them everywhere they could actually be wiped out."

Stephan didn't answer immediately. Instead he walked over

to a window and looked up at the sky. In a large sycamore tree near their building a pair of mourning doves had landed. Silhouetted as they were against the sky they looked remarkably like a pair of miniature passenger pigeons. At length he shook his head and sighed.

"Frankly, I don't see how they can possibly escape it if this slaughter continues. It may not happen in my lifetime or yours, but it has to happen eventually. They've just never learned to adjust to our so-called civilization like those two out there in the tree."

"But, sir, can't we get laws passed to protect them? Something that might stop that from happening?"

Stephan pulled his earlobe in obvious annoyance. "Tell me," he replied, "how do you convince *anyone* that a bird numbering in the hundreds of millions, perhaps still even in the billions, is threatened with extinction? This is a matter that I find hard to reconcile in my own mind, and yet I'm as sure as I can be that it will happen. Within a century, I'll wager, the only passenger pigeons still alive will be in zoos and nowhere else."

He shook his head again. "Well, better get some food and water into the pen and then we'll run these dead birds over to the lab. Remind me to have Felix start construction of an outside pen for these pigeons. I think they'll do better if they're not kept indoors."

12

ALTHOUGH the flock migrating to the north contained over three million birds, the passenger pigeon was one of the oldest of them.

At seven years of age he looked little different than he had during his second summer. His coloration, even to the willow-leaf patch of white on his right wing, remained the same and the only significant change had been one of size. He was undoubtedly one of the largest of this entire assemblage.

True, on some nights when it was damp and cool, waves of pain would emanate from the three lead pellets still embedded in his flesh — one in his right thigh, another near the base of his right wing and the third just under the skin in the center of his breast — and on such nights he would tremble a great deal and occasionally a whisper of pain would escape him.

Despite these handicaps, however, he was in excellent physical shape and there was no other bird in the flock anywhere near his age who could fly so far or so fast over such extended periods.

There was a pronounced eagerness in him to reach the nesting site, a familiar eagerness undimmed by the persistent tragedies — the repeated onslaughts of man and beast and weather — which had befallen him at other nestings. Yet the instinct and desire to propagate was an unquenchable fire within him and each new nesting season he was filled with new hope for the successful consummation of this drive. It was a fixed rule of nature over which he had no control and one he would not have altered had he been capable of doing so.

It was at such times, more than at any other, that he was consumed with the fire of life; when he could help bring into this world an offspring who might know a better life than he himself had found; when he could know the joy of self-inspired privation in order to provide for another; when he could watch with pride and satisfaction the swift changes from egg to hatchling to nestling to fledgling and, if they were fortunate, to a young bird ready to face life on its own.

Except for his first offspring — the little female he had sired and raised with the beautiful hen — this great drive in him had never been consummated. Five springs in a row fate had pointed a cruel and callous finger at them and the tiny birds that were so much a part of him had ceased to exist.

At the second, third and fourth nestings, men came and the tragedies of the first nesting were revisited upon him, except that on these occasions neither his squabs nor his mates survived.

During that second nesting, just to the southeast of Toledo, Ohio, his squab had been out of the egg only two days when, after the dawn feeding, he returned to find the woods resounding with gunfire and the terrified cries of young birds and old. And when he reached the low alder clump within which his nest was located, the nestling was gone and his mate was gone and even their nest was no more than a scattering of twigs on the ground. It was while he was winging away from this ill-fated site with a small group of other males in similar straits that guns barked from below him and the males began to fall, and a white hot pain burned in his own leg as a small lead shot smashed through feathers and flesh and came to permanent rest near the thigh bone.

At the third nesting, located in a great tangle of salt-stunted oak at the point where the long arm of Cape Cod joins the continental land mass, he returned from a feeding foray and found not the secluded nesting area but a vast raging fire of the undergrowth set by men seeking an easier and less involved method of taking the birds. Though he circled the entire colony twice, the spot where his own nest had been was now nothing but a smear of ugly white ash and blackened saplings stretching their naked arms beseechingly toward the heavens.

The fourth nesting, in that wild area of pines and birches and oaks in the Thunder Bay area of Michigan not far from Alpena, ended almost before it was begun. On the morning after the eggs were laid the men came at dawn, and once again the females were slain by the thousands and tens of thousands. And when he returned and settled upon his egg, which had become alarmingly cool, the fire of lead burned him again as the pellets ripped into his wing and breast and shattered the egg beneath him as he incubated it.

Last year's nesting, in the northeastern corner of Iowa along the Upper Iowa River and only a few miles west of the Mississippi, held more promise.

In comparison to years past, it was a small nesting — as all the nestings had become progressively smaller over these years — with perhaps eighty million birds nesting in a line two miles wide and six miles long. There were other, larger nestings in Wisconsin and Ohio and Pennsylvania and an extensive one of four by twenty-four miles along the north coast of Lake Erie in Ontario, and it was to these nestings that the professional hunters and trappers had gone.

Not that their own colony had not suffered at the hand of man, for indeed it had, but the attackers were relatively few in number and strictly of amateur standing, with neither the knowledge nor means of making their slaughter so generically devastating.

The passenger pigeon had taken a trim yearling female as mate and the baby, when it hatched, turned out to be a male, and the passenger pigeon was inordinately proud of this offspring. Together the two adults tended him and he grew large and demanding and had great promise of taking his place among the dwindling flocks . . . until the twelfth day of his existence when, during the night, the slim deadly form of a Bonaparte weasel snaked out on their branch as the yearling female slept over the squab.

She never awoke, for the sharp white teeth crushed her skull in one savage bite and only her spasmodic reflex thrust her from the nest to the ground six feet below. The male squab huddled, terrified, and in the next instant he, too, was slain, and the weasel ate a few mouthfuls of his brain right there in the nest and then departed to visit the rest of the squabs in this tree.

The stiff, cold body of the squab was still there the next morning when the passenger pigeon returned, and he murmured disconsolately for a little while before flitting from branch to branch, tree to tree, until he found a squab by itself which accepted the mass of food from his crop and relieved him of this pressure. After that the passenger pigeon left and he did not return.

And now, here they were, a flock of some three million, flying north above the Mississippi River in late February and passing within ten miles of the very spot where last spring's tragedy had occurred. But if the passenger pigeon recalled it, he showed no sign of it now. On the leading fringe of the flock, his wingbeats were among those which formed the pattern for this entire flock and he led them past this area without hesitation.

They flew low to the water, keeping equidistant from both shores, and since their front was only three hundred yards wide and thirty birds deep it became, in effect, a river of itself winding and turning a dozen feet above this mother of rivers and stretching backward for more than three hundred miles.

There was an ever-persisting danger whenever they passed the waterfront — or, for that matter, towns and cities anywhere — for almost immediately the shooting began from streets and rooftops, windows and balconies. Such target practice as this was great sport, and if the birds so downed were not eaten or otherwise utilized, what matter? They were like flies; you could never hope to get rid of them all.

Past La Crosse this flock flew and past Winona as well and between the great bluffs bordering the river. Only when they were a few miles south of St. Paul did the big passenger pigeon veer suddenly and flash up the mouth of the St. Croix River heading toward Duluth, and on the next wingbeat the leading edge of the column was with him. And in the marshy, barren tamarack area at the foot of the south range of the Fond du Lac Mountains, far from civilization, they settled. Here the trees were still leafless and the ground was frozen. Food was definitely not in abundance, and though there was enough to sustain this flock for awhile, there was not enough to raise young.

The leaders settled to earth in a forest of mostly red oak and pine and here they fed on acorns, while the tail end of the flock continued coming in. Even long after darkness had fallen and the earlier arrivals had long been at roost over a wide area, the birds continued coming in that steady stream. They settled to roost immediately.

The night air turned even colder, and shortly after midnight it began to snow. The flakes fell slowly, gently, but as the wind began to pick up and the snow increased, the flock quickly found itself in the midst of a severe blizzard. Time and again during the night the passenger pigeon shook himself to dislodge the mantle of snow that cloaked his back and he snuggled his head still more deeply into his breast feathers until he appeared to be a large fluffy ball with a pointed tail.

At dawn there were seven inches of snow on the ground and the storm, rather than abating, whipped more fiercely than ever around them. Flight was out of the question and the birds continued to crouch miserably on their perches throughout the day, and when nightfall came again the snow was still falling, though at less than blizzard intensity. By now the world around them was cloaked in white to a depth of thirteen inches. Since most of the birds hadn't eaten for twenty hours or more, they trembled ceaselessly throughout the night.

During the first light of morning the snowfall stopped and the pigeons roused themselves. A large percentage of them — mostly the yearlings — discovered too late the error of landing in this snow. Piled fifteen inches deep and in great drifts of seven or eight feet, it was like fine white powder in which they sank almost out of sight upon settling. This did little more than add to their discomfiture, but their exertions to escape the snow further exhausted them.

All day the flock circled over an ever-widening area in their search of food, but they found little. Even the normally shunned sumac clusters which pushed above the snow in widely scattered clumps were sought now and the bitter, virtually nutritionless berries eaten avidly.

As the birds settled for the night in the naked trees along the Bois Brule River a dozen miles south of that long southwestward pointing finger of Lake Superior, it began to snow again. The flakes were huge and soft and wet and clung tenaciously to everything they touched. The birds continued to shake them off, but before long their feathers were thoroughly saturated and they shivered uncontrollably.

It snowed until midnight and then the clouds abruptly broke and the stars shone with crystal brightness in the black of the sky above. But with the end of the snow came a sharp dropping of the temperature. By three o'clock in the morning the mercury had reached zero and about three hours later, as dawn broke, the temperature was fourteen below and still dropping. The wet snow had frozen into an iron-hard shell over everything and the pigeons were in a sorry condition.

The big leader shook himself and flapped his wings, slowly at first because his body ached from the night-long trembling, but picking up in tempo as the movement increased his circulation and warmed him. Having been in the van of the flock when it arrived here, he had been among those fortunate enough to find a good meal of acorns before the snow had blanketed the ground, but that meal had long since been digested and a powerful hunger wracked him.

Those that had arrived too late to eat were not so fortunate, for now the icy crust beneath the trees was dotted with hundreds and thousands of bodies of those that had tumbled from their perches and died. Even now, in the light of morning, the birds continued to fall regularly.

The large passenger pigeon shrieked, and his voice carried far in the crisp air and was answered a thousand times over. He flung himself from his perch and began to circle while those that could followed him. They were a pitiful percentage of the flock.

Three, four, five times, the flock of fifty thousand circled the trees, calling to the hundreds of thousands still crouched miserably on their perches, but they could not find the strength to follow. Those which tried were able only to flutter to the ground and then crouch there, colder than ever, awaiting the death from which they were too weak to escape.

The fifty thousand shot away to the west, and every pair of eyes scanned the ground ahead with great care for any suggestion of food. For an hour they flew, each wingbeat more difficult than the last. An increasing number of birds were sailing weakly to the ground, unable to fly farther, and each of these was as good as dead as he settled to the snow.

At the end of two hours of flight the column turned sharply southeast and flew slowly, its strength nearly gone and its need for food desperate. Finally, far ahead of the birds near a cluster of buildings within sight of the town of Sandstone on the Kettle River, the large passenger pigeon spotted an area of ground that was dark and he headed toward it with the flock at his tail.

High above the buildings — a farmhouse and three large barns — they circled once and then began to spiral downward. Soon they could see that the dark area against the snow was newly heaped piles of manure, much of it steaming in the frigid air. A large herd of dairy cattle stood in a fenced yard between the barns and disinterestedly munched hay from the broken bales scattered on the ground.

With their hunger so desperate, the birds discarded natural caution and funneled to the piles of manure, covering them so completely that only their backs could be seen, and the last to land alighted on the backs of the first. The piles were rich with food, mostly bits and kernels of undigested corn and wheat.

While normally the passenger pigeons did not prefer or even particularly like grains such as these, they would eat them in a matter of necessity and it had never been more necessary than now. At this point they would have eaten practically any grain available, no matter how little they savored it.

Many of the birds still having some of the bitter sumac seeds in their crops immediately vomited them to make more room for the waste grain and the flock virtually fought one another to get at the piles. Their feet were unfit for digging and so they pushed aside what they could with their beaks in order to find more. But while there was plenty to eat, there simply wasn't room enough for them all, and the overflow spilled into the herd yard where the birds scrabbled about the scattered hay, picking up the infrequent seeds that had fallen free and fighting with one another to get at the new piles of droppings expelled by these cows.

Although at first decidedly nervous when this cloud of birds descended upon them, the shuffling cattle quickly relaxed and continued feeding, looking at the birds occasionally, now and then accidentally kicking one when it got in the way.

A woman's voice cried out stridently and a door slammed,

and in a little while a youth ran out bundled up against the cold. He carried a shotgun, and when he reached a point where the birds on the manure piles were not in a line of fire that would harm the cattle, he floundered to a stop in the snow and began shooting.

Time and again he fired and at each shot a dozen or more birds died, but the others did not take alarm. Not even impending death could take their attention from this supply of food in front of them and they continued to gorge themselves. When the boy had fired all the shells he had brought with him and scrambled to the pile to begin picking up the dead birds, the living moved only enough to get out of his immediate way.

The boy was amazed at their lack of fear and then, as a sudden thought struck him, he dropped the birds he had picked up and raced back toward the house.

"Paw! Paw!" he shouted. "They ain't even flyin' away. We kin get 'em alive, Paw."

A stocky man, bundled much like his son, had come from the house while the boy was shooting and now he nodded and trotted off toward one of the barns. The boy intercepted him at the door and they entered together.

"They're gettin' two bucks a dozen for live pigeons in Chicago, Paw," the boy said breathlessly. "I read about it in that magazine. We kin make all kinds of money!"

"We ain't caught 'em yet, son," the farmer replied, flinging open the door to a twenty-foot-square feed room. Two full bags of corn and one of wheat leaned against the wall and dozens of other sacks, emptied over the winter, were tossed in a careless pile in the corner.

"Grab you some of them bags and come on," he directed.

The birds continued to pay no attention to them when they returned to the feeding area with their sacks. The pair began catching the birds without difficulty and thrusting them into the bags. As soon as one of these had so many birds in it that it became difficult to handle, the mouth was tied shut, the bag was set off to the side and the filling of a new one was begun.

For some thirty minutes the large passenger pigeon had been feeding here and now his crop, though not full by any means, had a comfortable swelling in it. A fear had been in him during the shooting but hunger had mastered that, and the man and boy thrashing about among the birds did not disturb him very much. A time or two he fluttered out of the way a little when one or the other drew unusually close to him, but this was more an instinctive reaction than outright fear.

He had pulled aside a cluster of material with his beak on one side of the pile and struck it rich, exposing a little pile of whole corn which had evidently been scooped from the floor along with the manure. His head bobbed up and down rapidly as he snatched up and swallowed the grain, and he became so engrossed that he didn't even know anyone was close to him until he was gripped tightly and carried struggling to the man and dumped into a sack.

Too late came the realization that he was in grave danger and along with the other half-dozen pigeons already in this sack he fluttered furiously until worn out by his exertions. Time after time the mouth of the sack was cautiously opened and another bird dumped in, and finally it stayed closed and he felt the solidity of the ground beneath the material of the bag.

The man and boy worked rapidly, speaking little, and they proved a good team. Bag after bag was filled with about four dozen birds and then laid aside, and as soon as small clearings had been made on the manure piles, the pigeons that had been forced into the herd yard fluttered over to the more accessible food supply in the piles to feed.

Only when two hours had passed and the hunger of the majority of birds still uncaught had been more or less appeased did the pigeons abruptly become nervous. They began to jump away and fly short distances around the piles before landing again when the humans came close. All at once a male similar in size, though younger than the big pigeon, leaped from the ground crying out a belated alarm, and the remaining birds followed him. They headed eastward and left behind them some nine hundred birds in sacks on the ground, victims of their own appetites.

The eighteen sacks were carried two at a time into the barn and placed on the floor of the feed room. When they had all been assembled the man and boy closed the door behind them and opened the bags. Immediately the birds tumbled out, took wing and slammed into walls and ceiling. Round and about they flew, screeching in alarm, and the air was filled with dust and feathers.

When all of the birds had been released the pair slipped carefully out of the door and ever so gradually the captive birds settled down. There were a number of shelves along the walls and every perching spot on them was filled. A few managed to retain precarious toeholds on the narrow windowsill, but most of the birds had come to rest in a mass on the floor.

Several hours later, after collecting and cleaning the birds that had been downed by the boy's shooting, the farmer and his son returned to the pigeon-filled room. The man carried a large bucket filled with warm water in each hand and the youth carried a large hog trough. The birds went into a frenzy again as they entered, but the pair merely set the trough on the floor and dumped the water into it. The boy left with the buckets and returned a few minutes later with them full again and these, too, were poured into the trough, filling it.

Immediately upon departure of the two humans the pigeons flocked to the trough to drink. Two days without water had given them a dreadful thirst and now the presence of the water seemed to drive them wild. The rim of the trough became solid with birds and still more landed upon those already there. Birds were forced into the water by the weight of others and in a very little while thirty of the birds had drowned.

With the immediate danger from these humans apparently past, the birds calmed down. There was quite a quantity of loose grain that had been spilled on the floor and become mixed with the covering of hay and the birds fell to feeding upon it. It was good solid food and, though not as much to their liking as beechnuts or acorns, they fed very well upon it.

Later in the day a prolonged hammering sounded through the barn as the man and his son set about building crates suitable for shipping the birds to Chicago. Since they could see no actual danger connected with it, the noise did not aggravate the birds too badly and they alternately fed, drank and slept while the heat of their bodies raised the room temperature to a quite comfortable level.

The large passenger pigeon squatted on one of the shelves and nestled his head on his breast. With his crop now solidly full, with more food and water available, his lot was not yet particularly bad.

But then this was only his first day of captivity.

13

A TELEGRAM received from Chicago, in reply to their own, somewhat changed the plans of the impromptu bird catchers. It had been their intention to ship the pigeons within a day or two, as soon as they had constructed crates enough for this purpose. But the telegram said:

ALL SEVENTY DOZEN LIVE PIGEONS AND MORE NEEDED BUT DEXTER PARK COMPETITION NOT SCHEDULED UNTIL MAY 15 WILL HAVE TO CAGE AND FEED IF BIRDS ARE SHIPPED NOW AND CAN OFFER ONLY ONE DOLLAR PER DOZEN IF YOU KEEP UNTIL MAY 10 WILL GUARANTEE PAYMENT OF THREE DOL- LARS PER DOZEN AND PAY SHIPPING CHARGES REPLY IM- MEDIATELY

The return wire was sent, and thus it was that for over two months the large passenger pigeon and his companions remained in their little room, well fed, well watered and miserable. The bird ached to spread his wings and hurtle along at high speed and his pinion feathers and tail were frayed with frequent encounters with the walls.

Acting instinctively, some of the birds during April picked

up loose straws and made feeble attempts at nest building, but it was hopeless under such conditions and with such material. The nests were always kicked apart quickly and the activity soon ended.

The lack of exercise and abundant food had caused the birds to become heavy and sleek and the large passenger pigeon, at the time of shipping, weighed very nearly as much as he had that day when he was a fully developed fledgling and his parents had filled his crop to the bursting point with food and left him forever.

Having become relatively accustomed to the comings and goings of the dairy farmer and his son, the birds no longer became so frantic with fear when they entered the room. In fact it had reached a point where they would sit quietly and allow a hand to be stretched over their backs, and their muscles flexed only momentarily when they were first picked up. After that they would allow themselves to be handled.

This made the job of packing them for shipment considerably easier. Since the youth had plenty of time to do it, he dismantled the hastily hammered together crates and constructed some unusually well-made ones. Instead of standard pigeon-shipping crates, measuring four feet long by three feet wide and five inches deep, in which six dozen birds were normally tightly packed and shipped, the youth made the boxes somewhat larger and even went to the trouble of compartmenting them with thin wooden slats so that each pigeon was in its own airy box within the crate, able to move about a bit and get fresh air but unable to damage itself in senseless fluttering.

A number of these boxes were built and filled with six

dozen pigeons each, and the big passenger pigeon was one of the last three birds to be packed, for he had continually outmaneuvered the reaching hands. But when these crates were filled at last, seven birds remained in the room. These the farmer butchered, and while his son cleaned and picked them he carted the crates to the depot.

Fantastic shipments of birds were arriving in Chicago and already the fifty holding pens at the Dexter Park Trapshooting Club were nearly filled. These pens were inside a long building similar to a brooder house and were actually more in the nature of rooms than pens, each measuring ten feet on all sides and equipped with dozens of sturdy perches running from wall to wall. One thousand pigeons were held in each of these pens and the crowding was so severe that frequently they piled deep on the floors and many birds were crushed or smothered.

The large passenger pigeon's crate was the last to be emptied into one of these pens and he felt a stir of excitement at seeing so many others of his kind. It had been a long time since he had heard the continuous murmur of tens of thousands and it was a comforting sound to him.

Many — in fact the majority — of birds in the pens were in highly disreputable condition. These were the birds that had been shipped in from widely scattered nesting areas by the professional netters and trappers, and little had been done to make them comfortable. Their feathers were thick and sticky with an accumulation of dung and many had broken wings or hobbled about on crippled feet.

Deplorable though they were, these birds that had finally

become housed in the trapshooting club's holding pens had fared far better than some. At the rail yards the mounds of dead birds taken from shipments that had come from too far or had shunted about on the rails too long grew dreadfully. Of just a single shipment composed of sixty thousand adult birds, more than two-thirds of them were dead on arrival at the terminal, most having died of thirst and crushing. The stench from their bodies was such that residents from as far as a mile away from the unloading yards complained, and the dead birds were shoveled into empty coal cars and hauled away to dumps.

For three days the large passenger pigeon was kept in his pen without food or water, and when finally he was removed from it with several dozen others and stuffed into a basket by one of the lads who worked there, he was rather weak.

The Dexter Park competition had brought gunners from near and far, and the grounds were filled with shotgun-carrying men who checked and rechecked their weapons, commented about the weather and the birds and the shoots of the past and made their wagers, which were such an important part of these events.

The actual shooting had commenced at eight in the morning and the cheers from thousands of spectators rose chorus on chorus as kills were made. Now and again there were groans when a bird was missed and then a spate of furious shooting as the escaped bird wheeled over the heavily armed spectators outside the fence and ran a barrage through which few birds passed unharmed.

The shooters were positioned so that when the birds were released the shots would be fired toward the wide expanse of Lake Michigan, bordering the east of the gun club property. This helped to prevent someone from accidentally getting shot and, by the same token, allowed the birds that were blasted out of the sky to fall into the water and float away, thus saving the club a cumbersome and distasteful job of disposing of the many carcasses.

The big event of this day was the shooting being done by Alexander Leward, who was attempting to break the club record set on May 15 in 1869 by Captain Adam H. Bogardus. On that date Bogardus had bet $1000 that he could kill five hundred pigeons in ten hours . . . and do all his own gun loading to boot. The bet had readily been accepted and just as readily won when, after shooting at a total of six hundred five birds, Bogardus downed his five-hundredth bird exactly eight hours and forty-eight minutes after he had begun shooting. This was such an admirable feat that it had become custom for the mark to be challenged during this competition.

Leward, as last year's champion, was today attempting to best the record set by Bogardus, but he was off to a bad start. By noon he had slain only ninety-six birds and had already missed over one hundred — all but five of which had been downed by the army outside the boundaries after Leward missed.

Shooting was going on at a dozen different traps but it was this one which held the most interest and around which there were the most spectators. It was to this post that the latched basket containing the large passenger pigeon was brought.

Leward was in a foul mood and, as his shooting worsened rather than improved as time passed, his mood degenerated. He cursed the birds for not flying as they should when released, or for pausing before leaping into the air, or for not flying at all because their feathers were gummy with excrement. These he shot from a distance of thirty feet as they scrambled along the ground in haste to escape, and he cursed each one individually as he did so because birds killed on the ground without having first been shot out of the air were not counted as scores.

A great many of the birds were weak and bewildered and even when the trap device sprang open and lofted them a few inches into the air, they often fell dazed to the ground and sat there stupidly. No few of these were fledglings less than two weeks out of the nest, and their tails and wings were not developed enough for better than a slow, straight-away flight difficult for any gunner to miss.

The trap was a curious device that had served this club and the hundreds of others like it around the country very well. It was a platform one foot square which was positioned atop a hollow post two feet off the ground. From the bottom of this platform projected a cylinder of wood which slid into the hollow post. Four triangle-shaped sides were hinged to the platform and, when raised, formed a little pyramid which effectively kept the pigeon contained. When the shooter shouted "Pull!" the trap boy would yank the long cord which

dropped the sides of the box and made the platform shoot upwards several inches to encourage the bird to fly.

On days like this, however, where the pigeons showed a
marked disinclination to fly, another device was brought into
use which rather effectively startled the birds into flight. It
was called Rosenthal's Mechanical Cat Pigeon Starter and it
was a clever device indeed.

This was a life-sized prefabrication of a large cat lying on
a platform on the ground several feet from the trap. If, when
the trap opened and released the bird, the pigeon merely
dropped to the ground and just sat there or started to waddle
off, the trap boy would pull another cord and the mechanical
cat would spring upright on all fours, its rope tail lashing.
Few were the birds which, if they could fly at all, did not
quickly leap from the ground when this apparition jumped
up before them.

It was two o'clock in the afternoon before the large passenger pigeon's turn came and he was lifted from the basket by
one of the boys and placed on the platform of the trap and the
sides were closed over him. Except for the little hole on each
side of the pyramid lid at the top, which provided air to keep
the birds alive in case a gun jammed and it was a long time before the cord was pulled, the darkness surrounded him, and
he braced his feet under him and shoved.

It was apparently to no avail, but just as he tensed himself
for another hearty shove, someone shouted "Pull!" and the
trap flew open, the platform springing upward. Instantly he
uncoiled his own muscles and shot away from the trap at high

speed, maneuvering in those erratic patterns he had learned so long ago in following the dark bird. A shot sounded behind him and then another, but now he was over the edge of the lake and instead of climbing higher he dropped lower to the water, and thus only those spectators on the very fringe of the crowd along the lake's edge had an opportunity to shoot. Fifteen or twenty guns barked at once, and blazing pain bloomed as one pellet streaked along his back, ripping out a swath of feathers and leaving behind a shallow red rut. More guns sounded and a half dozen or more pellets struck him painfully in the lower back and rear quarters, but not with enough strength to puncture the skin . . . and then he was out of range of even these shots.

He continued to fly swiftly and erratically over the water until the shoreline was low behind him and only then did he slow down and gain a little altitude. His back was afire from the wound and already he was dreadfully weary from his exertions. The only shoreline he could see was the one behind him, and so he continued flying to the east. A fearful thirst burned in him and he dipped to the gently rolling surface and came almost to a stop as he hovered with rapidly beating wings and scooped a minute mouthful of water. It was not enough, but the exertion of treading air was more than he could take, and so he continued his forward flight.

Far ahead on the horizon he saw a speck and he angled toward it. As he drew nearer it materialized into a large ore freighter heading northward after having delivered its cargo of iron-heavy rock to the smelteries at the port of Gary, Indiana.

[184]

His strength was flagging badly now and he lost all caution in approaching the ship. He was able to gain only just enough altitude to raise himself over the bow rail and tumble exhausted to the deck. He was more unconscious than not, and thus he was scarcely aware of it when the great calloused hand closed over him.

14

"WHAT'VE you got there, Tooley?"

The burly seaman spun about and grinned as the second officer approached him. He held the tired passenger pigeon cupped in his huge hands against his chest and looked down at it.

"A bird, Mister Simmons. It lit on the deck here. I think it's hurt."

Simmons's face was expressionless and his voice cold as he said, "And what do *you* intend doing with it?"

Tooley hunched his shoulders. "I ain't thought on it that much yet, sir. Guess maybe see if I could doctor it up a little. Looks more tired than anything else."

"We're not running a hospital for injured birds, Tooley, and you are not a veterinarian. Get rid of it."

"Excuse me, sir," Seaman Tooley said softly, "but I'm off duty right now. I don't see how it'd hurt anything if I was to use my own time fixin' it up a little. With the second officer's permission," he added hastily.

"I said get rid of it. Throw it over the side."

A flicker of anger kindled in the seaman's eyes and he held the bird out toward the officer. "Take a look at it, sir," he said. "He's too far gone to fly. Tossin' him over the side would be killin' him. I ain't got much learnin' but one thing my pa did teach me was to respect life, no matter what kind. Look at him, sir. He's hurt an' tired, but he ain't afraid."

Simmons looked down at the passenger pigeon in Tooley's outstretched hands but he made no attempt to take it. The scarlet eyes of the bird were clear and unflinching in their gaze and, despite the pain and weariness, he held his head erect. A vestige of a smile touched the officer's lips and then was gone and his gaze returned to the seaman.

"I told you to get rid of it, Tooley," he said crisply, "and I meant it. However," he added as the sailor's jaw muscles bunched, "I didn't say when, did I? Do you think you can fix it up?"

A huge grin cracked Tooley's face. "Yes, sir, I do. I don't think he's hurt bad."

"Well, do what you can and then follow my order."

Tooley watched the officer turn around and walk away and then he nestled the passenger pigeon against his chest again and went below. He stopped off at the galley where he wheedled a small bowlful of cornmeal from the cook and then he retired to his own bunk.

The first thing he did was to gently cleanse the bird's injured back with a soft cloth swab he first dipped into warm water. The break in the skin was not very bad, and when it was cleaned, a little salve rubbed into it and the feathers carefully wiped of blood, the wound was hardly noticeable.

He inspected with some interest the patch of pure white

feathers on the right wing, and then inch by inch he looked the bird over for further damage. His probing fingers found the tiny lump on the bird's breast which he inspected at length. With his straight razor he made a tiny incision over it, at which the bird tensed momentarily.

"Easy, feller, easy," he muttered soothingly. "I'm not going to hurt you if I can help it."

With remarkable gentleness for the size and roughness of his hands, he placed his heavy thumbnails to each side of the swelling and squeezed, and from the slit popped the tiny lead pellet that had hidden under the skin there for two years. The incision hadn't even bled and Tooley brushed the feathers back into place with his little swab and shook his head.

"Guess you're all right 'ceptin' for that," he said cheerfully. "Now let's see if you're hungry."

He poured some warm water into the bowl and kneaded the meal until he was able to form it into pea-sized balls. With thumb and forefinger he pressed the side of the bird's beak until it opened and then he put two of the food pellets in and the passenger pigeon swallowed them. Three times more he repeated this and now the bird began opening his beak of his own volition when the food was offered. As soon as all the meal was gone the sailor put some fresh water into the bowl and held it up to the bird. The passenger pigeon dipped his head and drank greedily.

From his seabag the man extracted a length of soft white cord. Expertly he formed a little noose, slipped it over the bird's right leg and tied it to his bunk chain, allowing enough

slack so that the bird might move about a bit on the floor and
even go into the darkness under the bunk a short way.

"I got things to do now, little feller. You just rest a spell
here an' we'll see how things look when I get back."

The bulkhead door closed behind him and for a considerable time the pigeon remained squatting on the floor. Finally
he stood and ruffled his feathers. He walked about stiffly,
stumbling a little when he reached the limit of the cord and
at last fluttered to the edge of the bunk where he perched and
hunched down comfortably. He slept very deeply.

It was several hours later when Tooley returned. At the
sound of the door opening the pigeon came alert but he
showed little fear. The seaman approached slowly and shoved
a stubby, extended finger under the bird until the pink feet
gripped it and perched there.

The food and water and rest had worked wonders on him.
No longer was there an aura of weariness about him and as
the sailor moved he spread his wings occasionally to hold his
balance. With his free hand the man loosened the noose and
removed it and now once again he cupped the bird gently
in his great hands and took it topside. He walked to the star-
board rail and stood there. It was bright and clear and the
water was a deep blue-green under the slanting rays of the
sun, rippled by a light breeze.

After looking around self-consciously and determining that
he was unobserved, the seaman raised the pigeon and gently
touched his thick lips to the end of the beak.

"Gonna leave it up to you, bird," he whispered. "You look

pretty good now. If you figure you can make it to shore, go ahead. And if you want to stick around and rest some more until mornin', that's okay too."

He held the pigeon higher and the bird swiveled its handsome head several times back and forth in little jerking motions. The lake air was invigorating and his feathers ruffled slightly in the wind, and suddenly the open expanse of sky and lake was too much and he leaped from the finger. He winged away rapidly thirty feet above the water.

A great delight filled him as he felt the power of his own flight and the rush of air past him. He had flown so little these past months! And now he was free again and before him stretched the world.

Twenty minutes after leaving the ship, when it was just a speck on the horizon behind him, he caught sight of the Michigan shoreline far ahead, but it was almost an hour more before he swept across the sandy coast and hurtled over a pine and hardwood forest.

Five miles inland he wheeled about in a tight circle and fluttered down to a little stream where he drank his fill. It was growing quite dark now and he took a perch twenty feet high in a hemlock. With greater care than he had taken since his capture in Minnesota, he set about preening his feathers, paying particular attention to wing and tail feathers which had become so frayed on their ends. And only the fact that he was not among others of his kind kept him from being as content that night as he had ever been.

At first light he was on his way again, flying northward,

and he had flown only half an hour when he saw far ahead a wavering cloud of birds. They were indistinguishable individually, but the pattern of movement left no doubt they could be nothing but passenger pigeons. The large bird put on a burst of speed and caught up to the trailing edge of the flight quickly. An exultant chatter welled up in his throat as he joined them.

It was by no means a large flock; probably no more than six thousand birds. These were the remnant of an abortive nesting just north of Battle Creek, in which some one hundred fifty thousand adult birds had been slain and the mortality among the squabs had been virtually one hundred per cent.

Now this flock flew with strong wingbeats to the north as if determined to leave behind the horribly implacable enemy who sought them out and destroyed them wherever they alighted. They stopped once to feed along the north edge of Houghton Lake, but as soon as the feeding and a brief rest were completed they were airborne again, and this time the large passenger pigeon had taken a position in the front line of birds.

As they reached the upper point of the Lower Peninsula the terrain below became familiar to the big bird. Here it was that he had crossed the Mackinac Straits shortly after he had found his fledgling wings, and now a faint memory of that undisturbed summer came to him and gradually he became the dictating factor of the flock's movement, leading them ever on toward the wild country of James Bay.

And when they finally reached this remote country to the southwest edge of the great bay, it was for the large passenger pigeon something in the nature of a homecoming. Here were the rivers he remembered and the forests. There the salt deposit where so many times he had gorged himself. This was where he had flown and roosted with the large dark male and there, in fact, was the very cluster of balsam fir in which he had awakened to the keening, lonesome laughter of the loon. And if a bird which spends most of its existence flying back and forth across the expanse of a continent can be considered as having a home, this was it for the large passenger pigeon, and a contentment he had seldom known enveloped him.

Much as he himself had been attracted to the mysterious dark male in this same country seven summers ago, so now a slender first-summer male in brown juvenile plumage became attracted to him and followed him everywhere. At first he more or less ignored the smaller bird but, as the persistent youngster continued to follow his every move, he came to look forward to his company and together they explored much of the area surrounding the foot of James Bay.

In late July and early August, when the annual molt began and the large bird started losing his feathers, prolonged flight was no longer possible. True, not all of the feathers dropped out at once so as to leave the birds naked, but for a period of two months there was a general replacing of the old feathers with new ones until, by the middle of September, each of the birds had a complete new set of crisp feathers.

It was during this period that the large passenger pigeon and his protégé spent most of their time on the ground within sight of James Bay. They still roosted a dozen feet or so high in the branches of fir trees, but the days were spent in waddling about, poking with their bills at sticks and insects, finding and eating berries and seeds and delectable young shoots.

Earlier in the summer, shortly after their arrival, the air had constantly been filled with a wide variety of birds, but the passenger pigeons were not the only feathered creatures undergoing molt, and by mid-August only occasional hawks and ravens, herring gulls and snipe and dainty little sandpipers still wheeled across the sky impressively.

There were millions of ducks in the area but by now these waterfowl had become wholly flightless and would remain so for about a month. And so the surface of the bay and its tributary creeks and rivers was frequently peppered with great rafts of swimming mallards and pintail ducks, with ringneck and black ducks and Canada geese.

Even the flying abilities of the spruce grouse and willow ptarmigans were affected, and for the predators it was a time of easy pickings. Huge golden eagles soared majestically on the wind currents, and though the pigeons watched them closely when they circled too near, they were not especially afraid. The eagles, while not contrary to taking a nice fat bird if one was careless, mostly concentrated on easy prey — muskrats and young beavers, deer mice and meadow voles and, most of all, snowshoe rabbits wearing their summer coats of tan.

Most feared by the large passenger pigeon were the gos-hawks. These were huge, fiercely taloned, hook-beaked hawks with great speed in their powerful wings. Unlike the slow-wheeling broad-winged hawks of farther south, these relentless hunters flew low, scarcely more than treetop-high, often within easy attacking distance before a grounded bird knew one was about. Their eyes were encased by a mask of dark feathers against light background, giving them a ban-dit appearance. And when one of these killers singled out a bird for his attack — whether snipe or grouse or rail or pigeon — that bird rarely escaped.

The terrible sharp-shinned hawks were feared, too, though not quite as much as the goshawks. Although their preference was for a diet of birds, they were hardly as large as the pas-senger pigeon and were mostly satisfied with dining on the myriad red-winged and rusty blackbirds, horned larks and robins and fox sparrows.

The four-legged predators, normally not too great a haz-ard, became a distinct peril during this molting period. Large gray wolves and red foxes prowled the forests and fields, mostly eating mice and rabbits but happy to devour any young grouse or duckling or plump pigeons they might sniff out.

Late in August, when the large passenger pigeon's molt was at its greatest, and his flying ability limited only to a vigorous flutter that carried him low over the ground for seventy yards or so, he and the slender juvenile waddled contentedly along the muddy bank of a little feeder creek. The young bird, already having undergone the worst of his post-juvenile molt, flitted back and forth across the rivulet, now and then startling tawny spotted leopard frogs into great arching jumps ending in little plops into the water.

One frog in particular caught his fancy as he waddled on the opposite side of the creek from the large male. Three times in a row this frog had watched the little brown pigeon approach and only when the bird was a few inches away did it jump into the water, kick vigorously in a wide semicircle and return to the shore a half dozen feet away.

But the little pigeon was not the only one interested in the movements of this amphibian. A pair of bright dark eyes watched it from behind a veil of reeds along the shore. The animal's muscles bunched in anticipation beneath its dark glossy coat, but when the little pigeon kept coming its attention transferred from frog to bird.

Closer and closer the pigeon approached and not until within three feet of the predator did it sense the danger and leap into the air. But the alarm born in its breast died in its throat as the sleek, five-foot otter sprang and snatched it back in one fluid movement. They fell to the ground together in a tangled ball of feathers and fur but the struggles of the bird were brief as the sharp teeth crushed the breast, found the heart and pierced it.

Normally a fish and amphibian eater, the otter was not above snatching an occasional unwary duckling or, as in this case, a careless pigeon. And even as the large passenger pigeon flapped frantically into the air on the other side of the creek and fluttered into the tall sedge grass nearly a hundred yards away, the otter had begun his meal.

The passenger pigeon crouched very quietly in the grass and even when darkness came he did not move. This was one of the rare nights during that summer when he not only roosted on the ground but roosted wholly by himself, and he was filled with a deep sense of loss and a penetrating loneliness.

15

MARTHA sat hunched on her perch in the spot that had become hers over the years. Her wingtips and tail were badly frayed, as they always were, from contact with the heavy wire mesh surrounding her and the other sixteen passenger pigeons in the cage. Even after each summer's molt, when neat new feathers replaced the ragged old ones, it was only a matter of weeks before they became ragged, too.

This was her tenth autumn of captivity and, for her, the worst time of the year. It was at times like this, when the days grew shorter and the nights colder, that flocks of birds would pass in the distance, and a terrible ache to join them in their unfettered freedom engulfed her.

During just this week alone there had been more than a dozen great flights of blackbirds passing over, and the faint chitterings that came from them as they passed over the city was a call to come, to fly, to join them, to share in that exhilarating experience of migration.

There had been other birds on the move, too, many of them. Even at night when the noises of Cincinnati faded to a murmur the sounds of them came: the muted rustle of a thousand wings high above, the occasional pipings of wild voices on high and once the stirring cries of a wedge of geese silhouetted momentarily against a wan full moon.

These were sights and sounds to break heart and spirit of a captive bird, and so she huddled deep in this misery visited upon her. Bad as they were, these were not the moments when she was most crushed; these were not the times when she would flail wildly back and forth in the cage, beating her wings frenziedly in endeavor to escape. Those occasions came with the coming of the mourning doves.

So like the passenger pigeon were they in silhouette that when they alighted on distant trees in the surrounding park late in the evening she often mistook them momentarily for her own kind, and then her harsh cries would rent the air and the others in the cage would join in the screeching, and all of them would flutter about and create a little windstorm in which scattered feathers would whirl and dip before settling back to the floor.

The doves would sit quietly on their perches for a while, perhaps one or another giving voice to the melodious cooing peculiar to the species, and then they would leap away and their wings would whistle distinctly in a way that never occurred with the passengers. At that Martha would resume her perch and sit quietly. Lately, even the company of the other sixteen passenger pigeons left alive with her here was little comfort.

Life in these Gardens had not been bad. Food was always in abundance, as well as water. Periodically the cage was cleaned, and every once in a while the keeper would reach out hesitantly and run a gentle hand down her neck and back. When she became sick, as she had on occasion, she was given medicine and made better, and in the spring quantities of fresh twigs were brought in and scattered on the floor of her cage as nesting materials.

During her second and third springs she had actually accepted one of the parading males as mate, and together they had built a flimsy nest and she had laid an egg. But the first time, there had been a late heavy snowfall and a sharp dip in temperature and the male had refused to share incubation. The egg had become too chilled when she was forced to leave it at last to feed herself, and though she remained on the nest for fourteen days it didn't hatch, and she abandoned it. After a few more days the nest and egg were removed.

The second time there had been an egg, too, but no nest, because someone had forgotten to supply twigs, but it would have made no difference because now she was the one who refused to set. This egg was also removed, and after that she never laid any more and the pompous exhibitions of the males in the spring failed to interest her.

And now, in late afternoon on this twenty-third day of October in 1895, she suddenly heard a sound that was a dim memory from the past. She straightened and craned her neck, cocking her head to one side and straining to hear better. The others had heard, too, and there was an interval of great expectancy in the pen.

The sound grew louder and now it was unmistakable — the rumbling thunder of thousands of wings; wings that could only belong to passenger pigeons; wings such as she had heard only during those first fourteen days of life as the adults alternately left in search of food and then returned with it.

Abruptly the flock appeared over the park to the north and within instants was passing five hundred feet above their very cage. The column was wide and dense but less than a mile long, and as it passed them by Martha and the others threw themselves about the cage in wild frustrations, beating their bodies against the wires, the perches, the floor. They screamed at the passing birds and it was a plea to return, an entreaty to wait, an anguished call not to be left behind.

The birds above them heard it and faint answering cries drifted down to the caged birds. They were cries which told the caged birds to join them, to come along, to fly high and free and far with them.

The frenzy in the cage became even worse, but the flock did not pause nor circle. Onward it arrowed to the south, to the land of warm breezes and salt-scented air and swaying Spanish moss.

In somewhat less than three minutes the entire flock was past, and the sound of their passing faded from a thunder to a deep murmur, from a whisper to a silence more agonizing than had ever been experienced by the caged birds.

Not in all the years they had been captive here had anything occurred to cause such frantic disruption among them and it took many, many hours for them to settle down, to return to their own perches and to sink back into that state of patient waiting for something they had never known . . . and never would know.

And on the floor of the cage lay five passenger pigeons, dead from their terrible exertions and having found the only release they would ever find from this endless ennui of captive life.

Martha returned to her position on the perch, fluffed her ragged feathers and sank into herself. And at the head of the flock, which had now crossed the wide Ohio River and was well into the northern hump of Kentucky, a large passenger pigeon flew in the leading edge, and the setting sun reflected brightly from the willow-leaf patch of white on his wing.

16

LARGE as it was, the northbound flight of passenger pigeons that arrowed out of Louisiana on the last day of February in 1896 was only a vestige of the great flocks that had once flown here. Where only a decade ago it had taken a much broader and deeper flock than this a full ten or twelve hours to pass over a given spot, now the entire flock crossed the Mississippi River in under two minutes.

The column was two hundred yards wide and just short of a mile long, and the birds flew in a single layer, rather than a dozen or more deep as in previous years. No longer were they preceded by that fantastic thunder generated by hundreds of millions of wings beating, for now they numbered just over two hundred fifty thousand.

Here and there across the Deep South a few scattered bands were heading north, too, but few of these even reached a thousand birds in number. This flock which now paralleled the river a few miles to the east over Mississippi's dense forests was the last great flock of passenger pigeons — a pitiful remainder of a once unbelievable population.

Even the face of the earth itself had changed, for now great expanses of forest had been cleared and grasslands had been ploughed and cultivated in neat squares and rectangles.

Few clusters of pigeons rose from the ground ahead to join the column and those that did seldom numbered more than a score. It was in one of these little groups that the large passenger pigeon dozed in a dead tree along the banks of the Big Black River just east of Vicksburg. The murmuring of the birds roosting here with him, rather than the sound of the flock's approach, awakened him. In years past it was always he who had been first to hear the migration coming, but his hearing was no longer as sharp as it had once been. At twelve years of age he was an unusually old bird; older by two years, in fact, than any other of the approaching quarter million.

He fluffed his feathers and stood, and though he was far and away the largest of his little group, the commanding figure he had once presented had faded. He stood not as tall or as lightly as before, and there was a faintly detectable drooping of his wings and even his plumage in general. The metallic gloss of shoulders and neck gleamed dully in the morning sun and the rim of bare orbital skin encircling each eye was traced with fine wrinkles.

As the flock drew nearer a touch of the old excitement gripped him, and he bobbed his head several times and flapped his wings, the white spot on his wing showing plainly as he did so. In other years he would have been first into the air but now he was last to leave the perch, and he joined the flock not in the van but toward the rear where the suction created by the flock ahead made flying a little easier.

Even then he tired quickly and dropped farther and farther back until he trailed the main body of the flock by a quarter-mile, a half-mile, a full mile. And finally, although they had been flying only a little over two hours, he was forced to glide downward to the edge of the Sunflower River near Clarksdale to seek food and water, and the flock was gone.

This was not the first time he had been left behind. All during the winter he had experienced it time and again as the little bands of younger birds he was with leaped from the ground and streaked away at great speed. At first he had tried to keep up with them and, at great cost to himself, had done so. But ever so gradually he had taken to dropping out when the weariness overtook him, and then there would be hours and days of loneliness as he moved about the countryside until he caught up with them or came across another flock and joined them.

Now, however, there was no other flock to join, and the loneliness was a deep wound which troubled him sorely. He drank his fill and ate what acorns and beechnuts he could find and then he slept in a feathery ball high in the limbs of a hickory tree. An hour later, refreshed, he fluttered back down to the stream, ate a little more, drank again and resumed his flight.

It was not at all difficult to follow the path the flock of passenger pigeons had taken, for their passage was clearly marked with speckles of their droppings. He found it was easier to follow the trail by flying just over the treetops, and it was lucky he did so, for just in time he spotted a Cooper's hawk diving toward him and he plummeted into the woods, maneuvering through the myriad branches at high speed and with much of the skill he had acquired in his youth. The hawk wisely gave up the pursuit in favor of less agile quarry, and after another few miles the old passenger pigeon landed to rest again. The escape from this enemy had taken much out of him, and it was another hour or more before he took wing again.

In a dense woods along the Coldwater River he saw where the large flock had stopped to feed and he settled to the area himself; not to feed, because he wasn't hungry, but because in some strange way it made him feel closer to the birds that had been here and gone.

His entry into this area of broken limbs and downed trees had not gone unnoticed, and from far off to one side there came the eager choppy call of his own kind and just as eagerly he darted toward it. He paid no attention to the scattered dead birds below him and landed lightly beside a pair of females who sat on the ground alongside a large broken limb. Both of the birds were injured badly. One could scramble no more than a few feet before collapsing in a little pile, her lower back crushed by the branch that had snapped from the weight of the pigeons upon it and struck her as she fed. The other bird had greater mobility, but one of her wings was weirdly twisted and dragged the ground and she could not fly.

The old passenger pigeon stayed with them the rest of the afternoon and at nightfall the trio huddled together against the protection of a log, comforted by the closeness of their bodies. But in the first light of morning one bird was stiff and dead, and though the other tried desperately to follow the passenger pigeon into the lower branches, she could not.

The older bird hesitated, reluctant to leave even this pitiful company, but the pull of the migratory urge was strong in him and at last, without a backward glance, he shot into the air and headed north.

The trail of the flock was a little dimmer now but still not difficult to follow, and he traveled above it as it skirted wide around Memphis and then turned sharply to the northeast. The wooded hills in this area of Tennessee had still largely escaped the ax and plow, and he paused for several hours in the wild land bordering the Hatchie River and there ate his fill of a plentiful supply of beechnuts.

It was after noon when he left there and in thirty minutes he was approaching the town of Jackson. He began to swing wide around it when there, in a cluster of trees near a domed building in the very center of town, he saw the sharp-tailed silhouettes of a dozen pigeons, and tossing caution to the winds he sped toward them. When he got within five hundred feet of them he saw his mistake, for these were mourning doves, not pigeons. The birds took off as he came near, and since they were considerably slower fliers than the passenger pigeons, it was not difficult for him to overtake them.

Though they were not his own kind, it was nonetheless companionship of a sort to fly with them, and he was disappointed when before even clearing the outskirts of town they settled to a newly spaded garden patch. He dropped down with them and for several minutes picked about half-heartedly in the fresh earth, swallowing an earthworm here, a grub there.

The danger was totally unexpected. One moment he was perched on a little clod of earth, his eyes half closed, and in the next there was a tremendous blow to his breast and he was knocked over on his side. The startled doves swept away on whistling wings, and the highly excited voice of a small boy pierced the air.

"I got 'im, Jimmy! I got 'im! Lookit!"

The two boys, one carrying a crude handmade bow, raced toward him from behind a large woodpile.

The shaft was stuck in his breast low on the left and it hampered the large bird as he attempted to regain his feet. Only when the boys were six feet away and the one who had shot the arrow raised his bow overhead to slam it down upon him did he manage to struggle upright and find his wings.

The bow struck the ground a heavy blow and snapped in half a fraction of a second after he was airborne, and he flew in a blind panic. The crude arrow hampered his flight severely and the pain was intense. Blunted by many contacts with the ground, the wooden point had become rounded and had penetrated less than half an inch, tearing the muscle fibers and causing great pain but hitting no vital organ. It flopped back and forth with his frantic exertions and with the force of the wind, and he had flown only a half-mile when the movement sent it sideways just enough to be struck a smart blow by the downstroke of his left wing and it tore free and dropped.

Loss of the arrow made flight considerably easier but the pain increased instead of lessening, and he set his wings in a long glide which carried him to the edge of a muddy little rivulet winding through a tree-bordered meadow.

His landing form left much to be desired, for his feet would not function properly, and he tumbled end over end on the bank. When he stopped and managed to get upright long enough to squeeze into hiding within a little pile of debris deposited by the last heavy runoff of rain, he was a most disreputable sight. One side of his head was a great smear of mud and his breast and back, too, were liberally coated with it. But the landing, graceless though it might have been, was decidedly fortuitous because it had forced a wad of mud deep into the wound, neatly plugging it and effectively checking the bleeding.

For six days, during the first three of which he had become progressively sicker and more fever-ridden, he scarcely moved. Had he not landed on this muddy bank in just that clumsy way, he almost certainly would have died. However, the mud not only stopped the flow of blood but, as he crouched on it, served as a coolant to his fevered breast and even somewhat as a medicant, for after the third day the fever left him and he was able to stagger to the water for a drink. The wound now began the slow process of healing, and on the fourth, fifth and sixth days, driven by a hunger that would no longer permit him to remain still, he crept about awkwardly, picking up a seed here, a cricket there, a fresh new sprig of greenery elsewhere. And while he did not feed well, he found enough in his immediate vicinity to sustain him.

It was a fortunate thing, for the weather had taken a sharp turn for the worse, becoming bleak and cold, filled with an icy, mist-like rain and even a few tiny flakes of snow. The raw air soaked his feathers and, when a cold gripped him, made him wheeze uncomfortably. The malady held on for three days and left him even less of his strength.

A week after that he actually flapped his wings a few times, but the pain was intense and he could not fly. He satisfied himself by waddling farther and farther upstream, concealing himself for sleep as best he could in the grasses and clutter along the shore. Another five days passed and the pain when his wings drummed was a dull ache that could be borne for short periods, and he managed to take brief flights of a dozen or so yards. More important, he was able at last to roost in the low branches of trees and thus be considerably less apt to fall prey to some prowling four-legged predator.

With each passing day more of his strength returned and his flights became progressively longer. During those days he meandered generally northeastward, and though he was forced to stop quite often for food and rest and drink, by the end of another week he was covering as much as five miles in a day. He crossed the Tennessee River near Danville but it was not until he neared Clarksville, one hundred miles from where he'd been shot, that he once more came across indisputable traces of the large flock of passenger pigeons.

Even though it was over a month ago that the birds had roosted in these woods and fed here, the ground and lower limbs were still coated with guano and here and there the telltale bluish feathers still clung to twigs or were caught in the bark of tree trunks or glued in place by the dung.

This was the longest that the passenger pigeon had ever been separated from his kind and he burned with a fierce desire to be back among them. His pace along their faint trail increased but was still extremely slow, for he seldom covered as much ground in a day as the flock had in an hour.

And then, on the sixteenth of April, forty-seven days after the flock had left him behind, he winged his way across the Barren River of Kentucky and found the remains of the nesting area of the passenger pigeons along the Green River in the vicinity of Mammoth Cave.

Remains were all there were, for it had been a doomed nesting from the outset. The birds had flown as far north as the Ohio River, but there they had met a severe late winter storm — the tail end of which had lashed the old passenger pigeon as he lay wounded.

A hard rain had turned into sleet, and the sleet into a heavy snowfall which forced the birds to the trees and ground over a wide area. For three days the storm continued, and on the morning of the third day the flock took wing and returned south to the area of Mammoth Cave where the woods had been rich with mast. Here they had fed and scouted and, since the flock was small and the food supply plentiful all over this countryside, within a couple of weeks the courtship had begun, the nests had been built, the eggs had been laid.

It was an unusually far south nesting, but it did not pass unnoticed, and when the wires came alive with the news the disgruntled trappers and shooters and netters in Ohio and Michigan and Indiana and even Wisconsin loaded their gear and entrained to nearby Bowling Green. When they arrived, a steady stream of wagons and horsemen converged on the nesting colony, surrounding it.

The initial attacks had begun when the nestlings were only two days out of their eggs, and the annihilation of this large nesting flock was inevitable. Not a single individual of the more than one hundred thousand squabs that had hatched lived to leave his nest, and less than five thousand of the adult birds managed to escape with their lives and flee to the north. This massacre had taken the men exactly five days, and there was much cursing and disgust over the small size of the colony and the amount of competition for the birds.

The old passenger pigeon reached the desecrated nesting area six days after the men had gone, and his first clue to anything amiss was the great swarm of buzzards gliding in effortless circles over the woods. The second clue to disaster was the ominous silence as he approached, and the third clue came when he was still a mile from the nearest edge of the site — the stench of squabs rotting on their nesting platforms. It was overpowering and filled him with a great fear. And in the woods where this carnage had taken place, the ground was alive with hogs rooting about, devouring the squabs that had been blown out of their nests by the shooting that had wiped out the community.

The old leader alighted only once in the area, in one of the tallest trees there. From this lofty perch he could see the remains of many hundreds of nests. Some of them had adult birds lying dead in them and virtually all held the bodies of squabs.

He was very tired and his wound ached and certainly he would have rested longer, but the grunting of the hogs, the sickening odor of death and incessant wheeling of the buzzards were too much and he flew to the north on tired wings, and the loneliness in him was even greater.

It was perhaps fortunate that he had approached the woods in the manner he did, for had he come in a dozen miles more to the east he would have flown across a great ravine where the carcasses of some two hundred thousand adult passenger pigeons had been dumped in profane piles several miles away from the railroad's loading depot.

It had been a decidedly bad year for the pigeon hunters. Not only had the nesting been small and the competition tough, but after all their work of killing and cleaning and packing these thousands in barrels, a derailment had caused the trains to be tied up, and when other trains had finally come in over a circuitous route in answer to the frantic pleas of the hunters, they had brought neither ice nor salt, and now it had become too late. With the ending of winter's last savage storm the days had become very warm and the birds spoiled quickly.

Yes, it had been a very bad year for the hunters . . . and a generic tragedy for the passenger pigeon.

17

In this year of 1898 there was not a man on the American continent — whether hunter or trapper, bird-lover or conservationist — who would have believed, if told, how low the population of the passenger pigeons had become.

The hunters and trappers and netters knew very well that they were scarce, of course. Last year was the first year in their memory that not a single nesting of passenger pigeons had been reported and their nets and barrels and wagons and traps had lain unused. But the birds would be back, they reasoned. You simply *couldn't* kill off a creature that had numbered in the hundreds of millions, even billions, as short a time as ten or twenty years ago.

And so, in their search for a reason, they theorized that the birds had migrated to Mexico, to Central America, to South America. There were so-called "authentic" reports of millions of passenger pigeons that had taken up permanent residency on a remote island off the Gulf Coast.

Even for the conservationists, such reports were more sure of acceptance and certainly far more palatable than the truth of the matter — that there were now fewer than twenty thousand passenger pigeons in existence and that practically every day this number diminished.

Because the pigeons were unable to change their pattern of life, unable to adjust to and make allowances for the depredations on their number by man, their population waned sharply. The fact that nesting in great colonies and low to the ground had brought them disaster time and again had not kept the birds from continuing the practice. The fact that flying in dense columns or clusters within easy reach of shotgunners had been the cause of the slaughter of millions of their number did not keep them from continuing to bunch close together in low flight.

They were, more than anything else, birds that badly needed the company of their own kind. Separated from such company in the numbers to which they were accustomed, they withdrew and seemed to lose all will to go on. When only fifty or a hundred or several hundred were together, they were edgy and constantly watched the sky and cocked their heads to listen for that great roaring thunder of wings that would signify the approach of one of the main flocks. And when the sound never came, when their numbers remained low, even the will to nest, to increase their species, grew dim, and though now and then a small flock would court and build nests and lay eggs, as often as not the isolated nesting area was deserted shortly after the eggs were laid.

It was in the spring of this year — the old passenger pigeon's thirteenth year — that this last concerted gathering of the species took place near the mouth of the Satilla River in southeastern Georgia. It had taken much out of the old bird the preceding fall to fly down here. His breast wound of a year and a half ago still tortured him with a constant aching, and the stricture of these muscles that had been damaged made flight more difficult for him.

But he was far from the only bird of this twoscore thousand whose injuries slowed him considerably. Many had broken, disjointed or even missing legs, some had beaks that were half shot away, a large number were missing toes on one or both feet and quite a few had become blinded in one or the other of their eyes.

And so it happened that these injured birds gathered and stayed together. When the flights of the younger birds were far and fast, they would be left behind to follow. But on the short flights — as most of the flights were during this Georgia stay — they managed to keep up and the birds remained rather closely grouped.

Even in the younger birds there was a more decided inclination toward keeping together, and when they would outdistance the older birds in their longer flights, eventually they would circle and come sweeping back and each time there was a joyous reunion, as if they were meeting for the first time in many years.

The winter along the sandy coastline and in the brackish savannah swamp country at the mouth of the Satilla was a pleasant one indeed. The weather was mild, less cloudy and stormy than usual and there was plenty of food. The ailing birds recuperated well in the warmth of the sun, and only twice during those months had their roosts been disrupted by gunshots and the flock forced to flee for their lives.

And now, in this gathering of the birds here early in February, there was an expectancy for what lay ahead. Perhaps this time, at last, the continued harassment by man would be ended and they could build their great communal nesting area in the wilds of Pennsylvania or New York State or Vermont or New Hampshire in relative peace. Certainly they were in numbers enough to rebuild the species. Given only a few years of successful nesting, it could well be that once again they would darken the skies in fantastic numbers.

It was a rather warm but hazy morning when the younger birds leaped into the air and began the great halo-like circling that presaged the migration.

Around they flew while more and more of the birds still on the ground rose to join them, and only when the ring split on the north rim and uncoiled in a long narrow line did the old passenger pigeon leave the ground and join the rear of the flock.

Perhaps it was in deference for the ones who could not fly very rapidly or perhaps it was just because they were in the mood for a leisurely flight, but whatever the reason, the leaders of the column set a moderate pace and it was not terribly difficult for the column to stay intact, even though it did extend in a very long thin line. The head of the column was scarce fifty feet wide and several birds deep, extending backward for some eight hundred feet, with the distance between individual birds increasing closer to the tail end.

The line left the shore and flew ten feet or so in height over the water where the breakers first crested and turned the water white. Past Jekyll Island they flew, and past Sea Island and St. Simons and Sapelo Island. Blackbeard Island was to their left before they had flown for forty minutes.

A large clipper ship lay at anchor in Sapelo Sound between Blackbeard and St. Catherines islands, and as the head of the flock raised altitude to pass over it, the decks erupted with gunfire and pigeons began to fall.

The uninjured leaders flared wildly and turned the column east over open sea in a great arc around the ship. Close to the rear, the old passenger pigeon had tensed at the sound of the explosions and watched the column far ahead. He saw a number of birds fall and watched the column make this abrupt eastward swing . . . and then he saw something even more frightening.

The head of the flock was disappearing, being swallowed up into nothingness as it entered a deep fog bank just off shore. The old bird shrilled a warning and veered sharply to the left, back across the beach of Blackbeard Island. The trailing end of the flock, perhaps two hundred birds, followed him; but the rest of the column trailed the leaders, executing to perfection the maneuvers of the bird ahead and just as neatly being swallowed up by the fog.

The dense fog bank was moving swiftly, and only instants after the last bird disappeared into it the ship became a ghostly shadow and then it too vanished. The memory of another great fog many years ago burned in the old bird and a constant trill of danger erupted from his mouth, and he flew with all the speed he could muster across the scattered savannah and sand islands, which finally became a sea of deep yellow grass as the birds moved inland. Soon clusters of trees were passing beneath them as the ground became higher and firmer, but not until they reached a long, unbroken stretch of pine forest did they flutter down to perch exhaustedly in the trees.

They had momentarily outrun the fog, but inexorably it came toward them, silently engulfing the clumps of trees they had passed by. Then it was upon them in a thick clammy blanket. An oppressive silence rode with it and the birds hunched together miserably.

Within minutes their feathers were covered with a fine sprinkling of moisture, and before half an hour had passed the moisture collecting on the needles and limbs of the pines was dripping to the ground in a steady drumming rain.

For the remainder of that day and night the palpable fog cloaked this chunk of earth and sea, and not until ten o'clock the next morning did the hot bright rays of the sun burn it away enough so that a degree of visibility returned. Even then it was well into the afternoon before the distant trees reappeared and the sea of savannah grass stretched out before them.

But the eyes of the birds that had entered the fog did not see the sun this morning. Almost instantly upon entering the fog their sense of direction was destroyed and panic overtook them. They circled and climbed and dived, striving to get away from this horrible enshrouding menace. Their feathers grew damp, wet, saturated, and it was a terrible effort merely to remain aloft. They began to drop in exhaustion and were clasped to the breast of the sea with muffled splashes.

At about the time the old passenger pigeon and his little flock finally left the pine forest in the middle of that next afternoon, the bodies of the fog-lost birds were being washed up on the desolate coastline by the hundreds. The herring gulls and black-backed gulls and laughing gulls swooped in and fought each other and screamed with insane laughter over the delectable carrion their carcasses provided.

The old leader and his band flew to the north, unaware of this tragedy and unconcerned about anything except following the instinct which drove them north each spring. They clustered together now in their oval formation and flew low to the ground with the single-minded determination prevalent in their species to get from here to there.

They stopped often to feed and rest and sometimes they managed to pass a day or so without being shot at. But usually there were shootings of one kind or another and each time more of their number dropped. And when they reached the area of Chillicothe, Ohio, they found a good supply of food and a secluded valley deep in the foothills where nesting could be accomplished safely. But now that they were here, they sat a great deal and muttered softly to one another and did little more.

Now and again a male would approach a female in a rather embarrassed manner, his chest puffed and tail spread, but either he or she quickly lost interest and continued to scan the sky and listen . . . listen for a sound of thunder that would come no more.

For several weeks they stayed in this area, and then they wandered toward the north and any thought of nesting was gone. A new drive gripped them and they headed toward Canada, where they would undergo their annual molt.

Maybe while they were on their way they would see and join a great winding flock of their own kind. Maybe when they arrived there they would find a vast population of passenger pigeons already roosting in the balsam firs and sailing in great clouds over the foot of James Bay. Maybe once more the wonderful, stirring, exciting thunder of the great flock would fill the air.

Maybe . . .

18

MARTHA was in surprisingly good condition for a thirteen-year-old passenger pigeon. She had finally learned the folly of beating her wings and body against the confines of her cage in the Cincinnati Zoological Gardens and since then her plumage had remained relatively unfrayed and unbattered.

She was one of eleven passenger pigeons still in the cage, of which only two besides herself were females. Yet while she took a certain comfort in their company she remained somewhat aloof.

Hers had become a peculiarly mathematical and mechanical existence. In the morning, three wingbeats would take her from her perch to the food dish where she would eat enough of the nuts and meal offered there to swell her crop slightly, but hardly half what the ordinary wild pigeon would devour at a feeding.

After eating it was three wingbeats more back to her perch where she would drowse for more than an hour, occasionally interrupted in her slumber by noisy zoo visitors who would stop outside her cage and stare at her and sometimes, if no one was looking, throw things at her.

[221]

For half an hour or longer she would flit from one end of her perch to the other, a distance of some fifteen inches, in a methodical system of jump–flutter–land–bob-head-twice–turn-around–jump–flutter–land–bob-head-twice. It was a monotonous activity, to be sure, but she always felt a little better upon completing it and it never failed to make her thirsty.

Four wingbeats to the water trough she would go next, dip her bill into the often stale liquid and drink deeply. Then four wingbeats back to her perch.

Even when the migrating forms of various species of birds flew over she didn't become too excited these days. True, she would bob her head a few times with a little show of interest and, on rare occasions, a sweet short note would whisper from her. But the only time she showed any marked degree of enthusiasm or agitation was when the mourning doves would alight in trees near her cage or feed on the ground a stone's throw away.

At such times a hollow keening sound would erupt in her and her head would nod sharply. And when the doves would finally whistle away on their narrow wings she would leap from her perch and fly a tight little circle in the air without touching the sides of the pen until she was too fatigued to do more. Then she would return to her perch and go to sleep.

Late in the afternoon she would feed again, rest on her perch until dark, drink deeply and then return and sleep until morning. Only rarely did this routine change.

One such occasion came about in early December of 1898.

The day had dawned with leaden clouds blanketing the city, and an hour after their food had been placed in the pen and the water changed it began to drizzle. All day long the rain continued. No one had remembered to unfurl the rolled tarpaulin at the top edge of the passenger pigeon pen and so the birds huddled closely together or against the base of the perch or along the back wall where the door was. But there was really nowhere to get out of the rain. The birds were drenched. Shortly after dark the temperature plummeted, turning streets into a fearful slick of glazed ice and causing the uncovered pigeons to tremble violently.

In the morning the discovery was made that the pen had not been covered and the birds were immediately moved into an inside pen, but the damage was done. Seven birds, including Martha, became ill with severe colds and by nightfall five of them had developed pneumonia. These five were dead the next morning, while Martha and the afflicted male hunched on their perches for several days, eating little, as their colds ran their courses. Their eyes became caked with mucus and glued themselves nearly shut, and they breathed raspingly through their mouths.

Both of the stricken birds lost considerable weight during this period, but while Martha finally took a turn for the better and the sickness left, the male bird grew steadily weaker. Six days after the rain, he too lay dead on the floor of the cage.

The remaining five birds resumed their quiet existence, watching with curiosity the people who looked at them with curiosity, eating their food mechanically, watching the silent sky regularly for the great wavering cloud of birds which never came.

19

THE Canadian summer had been a lonely one and the passenger pigeons had stayed close together as if to take comfort in small density of numbers. And when the molt had finished and they began their flight back to the south, only very rarely did two or three or a half-dozen passengers rise to join them as they flew.

They had begun the return flight with something less than five hundred birds and though between Quebec and Georgia they managed to pull another twoscore passengers into the flight, they were a sad remnant of greater days.

They flew over the trackless expanse of the sprawling Okefenokee Swamp, following downstream the barely distinguishable course of the Suwanee River from its origin, and only when they reached the marshy, pine-interlaced area west of Branford, Florida, did they glide to the sandy ground.

Although the flight had been unusually slow for a flock of passenger pigeons, the old bird was extremely tired. They had taken more than a week to fly from Canada to Florida, and yet it had been all he could do to keep up. On several occasions he had been left behind and had reached the flock again only long after they had settled to roost for the night.

Now that they had reached their wintering grounds, however, the passenger pigeons did not scatter in little groups of two or six or a dozen or so as in years past to spend their days feeding and exploring throughout much of Florida and south Georgia on their own. The tie that bound them together grew stronger all the time, and while there might have been a certain degree of spreading out during the day, they always came together in the evening to roost.

And always, always they watched the sky expectantly; watching for the arrival of that sky-blackening thunderous flock they knew must come as it always had. The vigil was in vain, and by mid-January, 1899, a heavy depression settled like a cloak over them and they drew even closer together.

This was the end of the old passenger pigeon's fourteenth year and he was far and away the oldest bird in the flock. His movements were stiff and weary and even the brightness of his coloring had waned, and the new feathers that had come in during the molt had an indefinable dullness to them, a lackluster that permeated his whole being.

When the flock made feeding forays to sites that were ten or twenty or fifty miles distant, he was always last to arrive and terribly weary when he got there. It was an extreme effort to fly continuously for more than an hour without stopping to rest.

Yet, it was this very frailty which served him now. On a heavily clouded morning late in the month the flock rose as one and flew northwest until, near Perry, at a great cluster of live oaks, they circled to land, only to be met with blasts from three shotguns.

Instantly they shot away, leaving behind only eight dead birds. But the fright of this shooting kept them aloft longer than usual, and by the time they winged over the Aucilla River the old passenger pigeon could keep up no longer. He landed on the river bank and watched the flock diminish in size until it disappeared from view. It was the last time he was to see any of these birds for several weeks.

He drank deeply, dipping his entire bill into the brownish waters and, when finished, ate some sandy grit from along the shore and spent the next hour searching out and swallowing a quantity of seeds from various plants and trees.

After resting for over an hour more after that, he finally took wing and flew in the direction the flock had disappeared. But the flock he followed had turned due west only a quarter hour after he had left it and had passed ten miles to the south of Tallahassee. Across the Ochlockmee River the birds had flown, and had landed only upon reaching the desolate shoreline of the Appalachicola River.

The old passenger pigeon, however, swung to the north around Florida's capital and from that day forward his was a life of searching, constant searching for his own kind. A lonely time it was for him, but since it permitted him to set his own pace in flight and stop when he felt the need to stop, it was good for him. He ate well and filled out, building up that reserve of fat that would help sustain him on the flight north.

Meanwhile, along the Appalachicola, the flock of five hundred had been joined by another flock of just over a hundred passenger pigeons that had come in from the northwest, searching as the larger group had for more of its own kind.

Several of these birds acted queerly. That they wanted very much to feed was obvious, for they constantly picked up seeds and other edible materials. But their mouths were coated with a slimy mucus and their tongues and the interiors of their mouths carried numerous cankerous sores. The swellings had so severely obstructed and constricted their throats that the only thing they could swallow was water, and even that only with the greatest of difficulty. And so, after mouthing a live oak acorn for a while, or any of the numerous seeds they picked up, they would eventually drop it where it lay amidst infected fecal material to be picked up and swallowed by another bird.

This sickness was the work of a microscopic protozoan that would one day be given the scientific name of *Trichomonas gallinae*, otherwise known as pigeon canker. Its effect upon the flock was swift and devastating. The disease spread quickly to the unaffected, and within only a few days hardly a bird there was not infected.

As the swellings became worse the birds weakened and were unable to fly. In a week their bodies had become severely emaciated. Those that had started the plague began falling dead on their sides following long hours of motionless crouching sixteen days after they were first afflicted. On that day twenty-seven birds died. These were followed by forty the next day and one hundred fifty-six the day after. The fourth day was the worst, when just short of three hundred birds fell to their sides and expired quietly. Although the cankers were ugly and painful, it was the swelling in the throats which killed these birds for, in essence, they had starved to death.

But now the worst was over and although there were a few scattered deaths on the fifth and sixth days, the remaining eighty-one birds felt the strictures in their throats relax and were able to eat sparingly of tiny seeds and soft buds.

Of all this, the old passenger pigeon knew nothing. He only sensed that as January had ended and already February was more than half gone, it was time to move north again, even though he was alone. Surely somewhere along the way he would meet that great cloud of his own kind which somehow he always seemed to miss.

Thus in the last days of February he commenced his flight to the north. He flew casually, stopping often for food and drink and rest, and so it was fully a week before he reached the Tennessee River at Florence in northern Alabama, where the course of the river changes direction abruptly from a due west heading until it runs almost straight north toward its junction with the Ohio River at Paducah.

Quite frequently he joined bands of mourning doves moving north like himself along this watercourse, but while they were company of a sort they were not passenger pigeons, and either he would eventually settle and let the flock fly on or he would continue flying himself as they dipped down to land.

Weakened by the disease that had ravaged them, the Appalachicola River survivors were more than a week behind the old passenger pigeon in beginning their migration and, though they covered considerably more ground each day than the old bird had, he had still made it all the way to the Kentucky-Tennessee line before they caught up with him.

The aged bird was asleep in the lower limbs of an oak close

to the river's edge when his eyes popped open and his head jerked erect. That faint whisper of sound could have come from only one source and he cocked his head and scanned the sky.

In a moment he saw them flying low over the shore, heading directly toward him. The weeks of loneliness were cast aside now as he stood high on his branch, flapping his wings excitedly. A piercing shriek escaped him and it was a sound which contained welcome and delight and an invitation, a plea to join him here for the food that abounded.

The flash of white from his wing caught their eyes and the desperate appealing cry reached their ears faintly, and they slowed, circled and then funneled down to the branches above him. They settled swiftly and then dropped branch to branch until they reached him and he followed them the rest of the way to the ground.

The acorns were thick here and beechnuts as well, and they fed heartily, slept and fed again. Tired though he was, the old passenger pigeon could not keep still and he waddled back and forth among the birds, listening to their chatter, brushing against them, seeing them, smelling them, reveling in their presence, knowing the excruciating joy of being among his own again.

They stayed here overnight, and instead of immediately flying at dawn they fed again before rising as one to wing north over the river. The old bird was in better shape than he had been for many months and the flock was in generally poorer condition, and so it was that now, for the first time in many a flight, the old pigeon gradually moved forward in the cluster of birds until he had taken his old familiar position in the leading edge.

The birds showed an inclination to follow him and so, at last, he had become a leader again, and the sense of this alone added strength to his wings. He brought the flock down often to feed and when, after crossing the Ohio River, they spotted far ahead of them the sparkling crystals frosting the edges of a salt spring in southern Illinois, they spiraled in for a landing.

There were doves on the ground here, not far from a large pile of reeds and grasses woven together in a bulky construction. A vague memory tugged at the old bird and abruptly he screeched out a warning and reversed direction and the flock followed him . . . but too late.

The blind erupted with explosions and a whole cluster of birds to the rear fell. There were more shots and once again the old leader felt the frightful stunning burn as a pellet thunked into his side and lodged there, stinging like a hornet.

The four men in the blind had hoped for but not really expected any passenger pigeons. Doves were their principal quarry now because it had been years since the big flocks of wild pigeons had come over. Some of the museums and many private collectors were offering good money for freshly killed specimens like these. The twenty-two birds they collected from the bare ground around the spring were worth easily five times that many dollars or more, and so they rejoiced and thumped one another on the back in glee.

When they had carefully placed the twenty-two carcasses

in a sack, they spread out and searched the ground more carefully and in the low marshy grass a little distance away found three more, and at each find they whooped jubilantly.

One of the older men suggested that the little flock had been just a scouting party for the main flock which ought to be coming along soon, and so they quickly propped up a half-dozen of the dead passenger pigeons in lifelike poses around the spring and retired to the blind to wait. But it was a long and fruitless wait and after three hours had passed they collected their birds and left, disappointed that the "big flock" had apparently gone elsewhere, but still pleased with their own good fortune.

The passenger pigeons that had escaped flew for the better part of an hour before landing again, and during that time four more of their number dropped out and were lost. They settled at last on a densely overgrown island in the Kaskaskia River not far south of Vandalia and here they remained for the rest of the day. The budding alders and cottonwoods provided food enough for them and they slept well hidden in the center of a tangled willow thicket.

The sharpness of the pain in the old passenger pigeon's side had eased a lot by morning, and though there was still a degree of ache to it, his flight was not affected to any appreciable degree. Four of the others were not so fortunate. When the little flock took off for the north at sunrise they were left behind, cuddling together miserably on their willow perches, unable to fly again now or ever.

And so, as they rose above the treetops and the sun shown

full upon them, the old leader set the flight pattern for the remaining wild passenger pigeons in America, for besides himself there were only forty-eight of them.

All of them were right here.

20

THE passenger pigeon was almost sixteen years old and he was alone now as he had never been alone before. Always during previous separations from the flocks there had been the knowledge that somewhere there were others of his species and eventually he would find them. But now, in early spring of 1900, as he crossed the Appalachians and winged across Kentucky, there could be no such hope, even though he couldn't know it.

For months he had sought his own kind. He had flown with doves and domestic pigeons and even with blackbirds and grackles for the sensation of company their countless rustling wings had provided. It was never enough.

There comes a point in the existence of every living species, if its population drops extremely low, when it straddles a precarious line. If things go well and the forces of man and nature refrain from dealing it further deleterious blows, it may survive and increase and over the years return to a semblance of its former abundance. But one little push over that line in the opposite direction seals the fate of the species. While the old passenger pigeon couldn't know it, his species had long since been pushed over this line.

The preceding spring several more of the birds in his pitiful little flock had been slain by hunters and collectors as they flew to the midpoint of Michigan's Lower Peninsula. But there were still more than enough to woo and mate, to build nests and lay eggs and rear young. There were food enough and places remote enough to easily hide this handful. But though a few of the males puffed up in preliminary courtship pomp now and again, none of the birds nested. Their time was taken up in nervous flittings about the state, seeking, always seeking, the great flock of their own kind nesting in a vast colony.

They were filled with a dismal loneliness that far outshadowed what desire they may have had for procreation. Life had always been a communal existence for them and so in their solitude they simply would not nest. Even when most actively engaged in feeding they would pause to cock their heads and listen for that distant thundering, and in the midst of night they would awaken again and listen closely, but the sound never came.

When they had flown over most of the Lower Peninsula without success, they crossed the Straits of Mackinac and flew westward through Upper Michigan and into Wisconsin. They found only occasional gunners who shot at them and predators which attacked them and when, far above Minnesota in the Lake of the Woods country, they paused for their summer molt, only thirty-two of them remained.

During the height of the molt a terrible storm had come and for three days the skies had alternately broken loose in deluge and eased to steady drumming rain. The creeks and rivers had filled and then overflowed. The flock was caught on the ground and the soaking had worked with the molt to make the birds wholly incapable of flight, and they had pressed together on the ground in a miserable mass as the waters lapped about their bellies. And when the storm had ceased, so too had the lives of twenty-one passenger pigeons. Only those — the old bird among them — that had found slightly higher tussocks of grass and had not actually lain in the water survived.

The summer had passed and autumn came and with it the flight south. A cat took a bird here, a hawk snatched one there, a gun brought down two elsewhere and inevitably their numbers were whittled away. And when just three weeks before, they had turned their backs on the south and resumed the gradual search to the north, only three passenger pigeons flew with the old bird. All of them were males.

Two of these had been lost in flight as the quartet cruised low over the pecan groves of central Georgia and the twin crashing of a double-barreled shotgun brought down dinner for a sharecropper. And two days after that the old bird's sole companion, a slim three-year-old male, had been struck by a huge duck hawk neither of them had even seen prior to its attack and had fallen in a cloud of feathers, while the old bird dived low and wheeled erratically through a thickly wooded mountain slope.

So now, in the spring of 1900, he was alone, and his head moved back and forth constantly as he flew, always searching the horizon for that wonderful cloudlike flock which existed only in his memory.

He roosted for the night on the Kentucky side of the Ohio River a dozen miles downstream from Portsmouth, and on the morning of March 24 he flew low across the wide Ohio, climbed over the rolling hills and glided into Ohio's Scioto River valley.

He flew steadily, if slowly, stopping twice to rest, though not to eat. Just after he had crossed from Scioto County into Pike County and was several miles from the little town of Sargents, he swooped into a cluster of oaks and hickories along the east bank of the Scioto to feed.

His selection of feeding area was unfortunate. He never even noticed the little boy who crouched motionless behind a log fifty feet away, gripping in his hands his Christmas present of exactly three months ago — a BB-gun.

In that interval the boy had shot many hundreds of the little BB's with it and had become remarkably accurate with it at distances up to thirty feet. He had downed field mice and sparrows and chickadees and on this day, while walking along the banks of the river, had added several tiny frogs — spring peepers — to his list of victims.

It was just a short distance from here that he had spotted a nervous little chipmunk as it disappeared into a hole at the base of a butternut tree and so he had positioned himself in readiness here for when this bigger game should reemerge.

The little striped rodent had indeed come out again very quickly and stood on the little mound of earth beside the hole, its tail jerking repeatedly as it tested the air and looked about with big bright eyes for possible enemies. And just as the youngster's finger had started to squeeze the trigger, the chipmunk had given a little high-pitched twitter and vanished into the hole again. It had been frightened by the arrival of the passenger pigeon.

His eyes having been on the chipmunk, the boy hadn't seen the bird land, but the disappointment in his face turned to eagerness when he caught the flash of white on the bird's wing as it dropped from branch to branch.

The passenger pigeon landed in the old dead leaves fifty feet from the boy, who had remained frozen, his little air rifle still to his shoulder and pointed generally in that direction. Slowly, ever so slowly, the feeding of the bird brought it closer.

Forty feet ... thirty-five ... thirty ...

Now he was within range but still the boy didn't move, and the old bird didn't know he was there.

Twenty-five feet ... twenty ... fifteen ...

With infinite slowness the boy brought the gun to bear on that proud old head; the head that the bird paused to lift high every now and then to scan the silent sky and listen. It was during such a pause that the boy's finger pressed the trigger and the gun popped softly and a little ball smaller than a pea left the muzzle.

For the old bird there was a flash of brilliant light as the tiny round pellet slammed through his eye and came to rest in his brain. And in that fractional instant before he died, the old passenger pigeon may have heard the gust of wind which swept through the tops of the trees with a sound not unlike the murmur of a million distant wings.

EPILOGUE

THE *pride of the little boy who had shot the passenger pigeon was boundless as he handed over the carcass to* Mrs. *Barnes and asked her if she'd like to have it to mount, since taxidermy was her hobby.* Mrs. *Barnes, wife of the former sheriff of Pike County, accepted it gratefully. Although she was an amateur at the business, she did quite a laudable job in mounting the specimen, even though for its eyes she used shiny black shoebuttons. Later she donated it to the Ohio State University in Columbus, where it remains today in dusty solitude. This was the last authenticated sighting of a wild passenger pigeon in the world.*

After many years of extensive research and study, Professor A. W. Schorger of the University of Wisconsin wrote in The Passenger Pigeon: Its Natural History and Extinction:

There is a specimen in the Ohio State Museum, killed by a boy March 24, 1900, near Sargents, Pike County, and mounted by Mrs. C. Barnes... The authenticity of the record [as the last of the wild passenger pigeons] has never been questioned at Ohio State University. In view of all the information available, it is believed that the record should stand.

[241]

But though this was the last wild passenger pigeon, what of Martha and the other passenger pigeons in the Cincinnati Zoo? Well, Martha's life remained unchanged. She ate, she drank, she slept, she perched. And she listened. Day after day, week after week, as the months became years and the years became decades, she listened ... but the wonderful roaring of that multitude of wings had become a thunderous silence.

In 1900, about the time the old passenger pigeon was killed, only three of the birds remained alive in the Cincinnati Zoological Gardens; two males and Martha. In April of 1909 one of these males died and the remaining male now took to perching close to Martha for companionship. But the loneliness was an awful thing and he became ever more frail until, on July 10, 1910, he too died and, with him, any remote hope that their number might increase.

And now Martha was alone. Alone in a way that can be described but never fully appreciated, for she was the last ... the only living creature of her species in the world. For over four years longer she lived in isolation in her cage.

At 12:45 P.M. on September 1, 1914, her head sagged and she trembled. And then, without ever having known the joys of hurtling through the heavens at great speed; without ever having flown on her powerful wings more than ten feet in any one direction; without ever having experienced that gratifying and necessary function of raising one of her own young to maturity; without ever having known the true meaning of freedom, Martha fell from her perch very quietly and lay dead.

And with the passing of Martha, the passenger pigeons became extinct from the face of the earth.

Martha's body was discovered by the director of the zoo at 1 P.M. Acting on a promise made years earlier, he suspended the body of the bird in water and froze it whole until it was encased in a three-hundred-pound block of ice. Shipped immediately to the Smithsonian Institution in Washington, D.C., it arrived September 4, and a highly detailed anatomical examination of the body was made.

After that, Martha was mounted. She now perches behind glass in the U.S. National Museum, a perpetual reminder of the thoughtlessness and greed of mankind. A label at her case reads:

Ectopistes migratorius (Linnaeus)

PASSENGER PIGEON

LAST OF ITS RACE. DIED AT CINCINNATI

ZOOLOGICAL GARDENS, SEPTEMBER 1ST, 1914.

AGE 29 YEARS

PRESENTED BY THE CINCINNATI ZOOLOGICAL

GARDENS TO THE NATIONAL MUSEUM

ADULT FEMALE, 236,650

Printed in the United States
21154LVS00002B/77